Paper Hearts

Georgia Harris

Contents

01 | spark

Renting an apartment together was quite possibly their best, and worst, idea to date. Ellie and Micah wondered what was going through their heads when they purchased the two-bedroom apartment, separate office and all. He had his man den, and she had her home theater, and, most importantly, they had each other. The lingering scent of year round peppermint was a grounding force for Micah - a reminder of how lucky he was to have his best friend as a roommate. The sweaty shorts left lying on the floor were a friendly reminder to Ellie that no matter how disgusting Micah was, she would trade anything in the world to keep him by her side.

They were what others called accidental friends. Their friendship was the by-product of two disastrous relationships coincidentally coinciding. Ellie's boyfriend, Gavin, had been best friends with Micah's girlfriend, Hannah, unbeknownst to either of the current friends. Both relationships had been sailing calm seas, listing to the lull of the waves against the helm of the boat, but neither noticed the tempest in the distance. Small suspicions got caught in the water, getting tossed and turned in the whirlpool of raging emotions, resurfacing as bitter arguments. Sutures from their brash encounters hung limp on their skins, wounds not closing completely, never scarring correctly.

An accumulation of arguments resulted in fragile relationships, weathered to nothing more than an inkling of infatuation - whatever the relationship started as. It was in the grand scheme of things that both the relationships come to an end, but not in the way that they did. Not with Gavin and Hannah trying to surreptitiously dive under the covers to hide their stark naked bodies, or with Micah nearly grabbing Gavin by his balls to throw him out the window. Definitely not with Micah calling Ellie up in the middle of the night to ask her to share his six-pack of beer with him. But perhaps that was also in the best interest of the grand scheme of things - rearranging two mismatched pairings to create a new set of optimal relationships essential to producing the most beautiful babies.

Micah was always on Ellie's case for dating men only because of their looks and their chances of giving her Channing Tatum look alike's - in Ellie's defense (something she really didn't have), she claimed that she was always willing to learn to love someone.

Unfortunately for Gavin and Hannah, their relationship didn't last. In theory, once a cheater, always a cheater - Micah had given the duo three weeks while Ellie had been more lenient, giving them two months. Both hypothesized that it wouldn't be the cheating to create the rift in the relationship, but the paranoia of future possibilities. Ellie had run into Gavin at the local coffee shop a month after he made his relationship with Hannah official - his Facebook status finally read In a Relationship. Eyes bloodshot and head throbbing, he warily explained the demise of his relationship - said something about sharing a coffee one last time before moving out.

Ellie didn't care. Micah wasn't humored. And neither shied away from publicizing their own relationship status - it wasn't big enough for Facebook, but it was worth mentioning to some unworthy exes. Moving in together was a surefire way to garner jealousy in the eyes of even those with the best masks.

So while one of life's seemingly destined matches faced the final chapter of its love story, there was one match that hadn't even started its story. Micah and Ellie were blissfully aware of the tension between the two - dehydrating sexual tension - but were unnaturally reluctant to act upon it. They were in no rush to jeopardize the greatest of friendships for some casual sex that could easily turn messy - literally and figuratively. For the both of them, the tension was leashed by stolen glances, lingering smiles, and fleeting touches. It was kindled by the knowledge that a flame couldn't go out without being started in the first place.

The first spark was struck.

As long as they continued to fight the tension, the fire would be contained to its square of space and the forest leaves would never feel the sensation of crisp heat, but once passion overwrote every other sense...

Micah would be the fire and Ellie the forest; she would be all his to burn.

• • •

Friday's were always Ellie's favorite days. It was the only day of the week where she had a morning shift at the clinic over the afternoon. Finishing errands first thing in the morning gave her plenty of time to relax when she returned to an empty house - clean, quiet, and totally void of the talkative Micah. As much as she loved having him around, there was no getting any actual work done in his presence. Often, he joined her at the kitchen table where she worked - propping his own laptop on his lap and leaning far back, far enough that his foot could tickle hers. That in itself was plenty a distraction.

It wasn't being tickled by Micah that was the problem; it was being around him.

His small smiles had her heart stuttering and his gaze followed her everywhere she went. It was a usual occurrence that his eyes would travel down the slope of her body whenever she stood to get water. Liquid lodged in the back of her throat as he fixated his eyes on the small of her back, then the swell of her ass. Sometimes, Ellie thought of taking water to him - maybe it would help in quenching his own thirst - but she never had the courage. Bringing him water meant she was acknowledging his stares, and she feared that if she made it clear that she did, in fact, notice, things would be awkward between them.

Yet another reason why it was a terrible idea for them to move in together - Micah was always dreaming about that ass pressed against him, and Ellie was always wondering what he would do if she gave in to whatever he desired. But for every negative, there was always a positive, and for Ellie, it was that Micah was her inspiration. The longer his eyes stayed put, the further his hands roamed, the more she fantasized - the more she had to put on paper.

As a part-time author, writing sex wasn't difficult for Ellie; it was the tension leading up to the sex that she struggled with. It was the accidental brush of a hand against a bulge, the sudden graze of lips against the collarbone, the slip of a hand between the legs that Ellie had a hard time envisioning. That particular hunger was always in Micah's eyes; in Ellie's too - she just had a better way of hiding it. Unfortunately, she'd become so used to pushing down her desires that she no longer knew what it was like to express them.

Or release them.

Micah emerged from the bathroom with a shout, hair wet and chest bare, snapping Ellie out of her thoughts. Her laptop was shut and tucked neatly under her pillow just as he entered her room. Without knocking.

"About time," she said, kicking off her bed. "I'm starving."

"You didn't have to wait," he pointed out, shuddering when Ellie slapped a hand over his stomach to push him out of the way. Micah had a bad habit of leaning against the doorframe. Given his broad shoulders, he almost never left her room to enter or leave. There was also no magical word for him - either you stayed put, or you made him move. For Ellie, even if she put all her weight into shoving him, he never budged. It was like a wave crashing into the edge of a cliff - with every subsequent splash, the cliff weathered, but it didn't go anywhere.

Ellie had long given up on shoving Micah out of the way.

"Are you going to move or are we going to just stand here all night instead of eating?"

"What's for dinner?"

Ellie pressed her lips together. "Pizza." A kiss on his cheek. "With jalapenos." A breath against the shell of his ear. "And bacon."

"Goddamn do you know the way to my heart." A hand reached up to tug her bottom lip out from between her teeth. He looked like he wanted to catch it with his own. "I love you so much for that."

"Say that again."

Micah yanked her close, his grip around her waist crushing. "I love you so fucking much, Ellie."

Ellie searched his eyes for something - anything - but his mask had gotten better with time. Whatever he was thinking, his eyes betrayed nothing. "And how do you mean that, Micah?"

He winked. "I mean it however you want me to mean it."

• • •

a/n: i think this'll be the regular length for chapters - around 1-1.5K words. what do you guys think of ellie and micah so far? thank you to everyone who read the last chapter - your support meant the absolute world! so, as i said, this story will contain mature scenes but some chapters will be tamer than others - this is one of the tamer chapters if you couldn't tell already. i hope you all enjoyed! i'm thinking of making this about 20 parts or so, so this shouldn't be too long. i hope school - or the election smh - isn't putting anyone in shock just yet. i won't be online all of next week (most likely) because i'll be travelling so everyone have a wonderful thanksgiving! i hope to talk to y'all soon in a later update. again, thank you guys so much for the support! <3

02 | finite

PAPER HEARTS | 02

Isla Evans loved Micah Matthews with the entirety of her heart, with every fiber of her being. He owned her, completely and wholeheartedly, but more often than not she got the feeling that she would never have Micah the way he had her. His attention would always be divided - a quarter going to her and the rest going to Ellie Harte.

He was unnaturally good at rooting out any seeds of doubt Isla planted in her head - she had yet to catch onto his methods. For every time Isla caught his gaze lingering on Ellie for too long, Micah made sure to feather enough kisses along her collarbone to dispel any and all of her thoughts. Whenever she thought Micah was standing too close to Ellie, he made sure to stand even closer to Isla - just until he started to pulse against her, until she could feel her sudden warmth radiating against his skin.

She took his bait without a question only as long as he continued to treat her like he wanted her.

What Isla and Micah had was, in fact, love - just misguided.

Love was a violent flutter in the chest, a sudden loss of breath; when someone was so lost in the confinements of depending on someone else, that they lost the mental capacity to think for themself. It was a bug - a disease without a cure. Infectious as it passed through the air in wisps, it destroyed from the inside but embraced from the outside. Infinite was when love ran bone deep, rippling through hearts from the core.

More often than not, love was finite.

It was halted by dirty secrets and superficial interests. It reached an impasse as truth and trust held onto each other by a worn thread. With the lies so rooted into the foundations, sweet nothings floated into space. What were promises when they were filled with nothing but weightless words?

• • •

There was one benefit to Ellie working the afternoon shift at the clinic: she wouldn't be around to see Micah take Isla to his bedroom nor would she be around to hear all the things he did to Isla. He didn't need her knowing that while he talked to Isla, he was thinking of her; thinking of asking her how work was, if she needed a head massage, what she wanted to do before bed. He didn't need her knowing that he was always thinking of running his hand through her silken, blonde hair, flicking her button nose until her lips pulled into a half-smile half-grimace.

He didn't need her knowing what she did to him.

Micah had thrown his shirt aside and had propped his arms behind his head as he leaned against the bed's backboard. He watched intently as Isla wandered around the bathroom, the door cracked open, in nothing more than her bra and panties. She ran a hand over the love bites along the hollow of her neck and the swell of her breasts. Her fingers moved deftly, putting pressure wherever the purple-red polka dots blossomed on her skin.

Her face popped up in the doorframe. "You really need to lighten up with the rough play."

He flashed her a coy smile. Micah beckoned her forward with the tilt of his chin, and whenever he called, Isla always came. Micah wrapped an arm around her naked waist as she neared the bedside. She squealed as she fell into his lap, hands braced on his chest as he cradled the back of her head. Isla tried to pull away, but he only tightened his grip. "I thought you liked it," he murmured against her chin.

"Not the aftermath." Isla's head tilted back, giving Micah better access.

"Don't lie. You like that too."

"Fine, I like that too. I just don't like cleaning up the mess you make."

His voice was husky. The mischievous smile was back. His fingers hooked around the waistband of her underwear. "Then let me clean it up myself."

Isla twisted, pressing her back flush against his chest. Her hair was still damp from the shower she'd taken earlier and the cold water against his warm skin was enough to make him shudder against her. She must've mistook his shiver for pleasure because she ground her hips, quickly and subtly against his. Micah's resolve was quick to dissolve - when she drew her hair out front, his lips were already occupying the freed space. Isla's hands roamed, struggling with his belt buckle. Micah was still in his work clothes, but he wasn't worried about staining them - he couldn't worry.

"I've been craving you all day, you know that?" he groaned. His teeth snagged her earlobe; his tongue followed to tickle the sweet spot behind her ear. Isla had managed to rip his belt free of its loop and her fingers were hooked in one of his pockets. Her bra clasp popped open, the silken material falling in a pool at her tucked feet. Somehow, while he'd been focused on sponging kisses down her neck, collar, arm, he'd slipped her underwear off. Isla's free hand slipped between her thighs.

She turned to straddle him. He was hard against her bare skin - painfully hard. Micah let his eyes flutter when her mouth began to move. Her tongue left a wet trail down his abdomen, pausing at the button of his pants. When Isla looked at him, up and over her lashes, he swore - her dark blue eyes were radiant and undoubtedly hungry. "How will you ever curb that craving?"

"You know very well how." He barely managed to bite out the words - she was already dragging his pants down the length of his legs.

"Say the words, Micah."

He eased her onto her back, his chest pinned against hers. His head swooped down to capture her breast in his mouth, and a moan slipped past her lips. She bucked against his naked body, now that she had finally managed to slip his boxers down to his ankles. "I'm going to fuck you hard, Isla."

"How hard?"

Micah flipped her onto her knees, knocked her legs apart to give himself ample room. When he fisted her hair and pulled, the wicked smile playing on her lips was almost enough to throw him over the edge. "So hard that for tomorrow and every day following, your lips will only be able to say one word."

"What word?"

"Micah."

With Isla, it was only ever rough, carnal sex. It was Micah pounding her ass and her screaming his name into the pillow until her voice was hoarse. Isla liked it when he started off short, fleeting - building up to slow, long, powerful thrusts - ones strong enough to reverberate through her body. It was always her talking dirty, him slapping her ass until it was red, and her taking him in her mouth until they both had nothing else to give. Isla always equalled toe-curling sex that left them both numb even the next morning.

It would've been different with Ellie. She would've liked to take it slow - a proper build up for a complete climax.

"Harder, Micah," Isla hissed.

"That would mean breaking you."

He paused with his thrusts, letting her catch her breath. "Then I want you to fucking destroy me."

Perhaps nice, quick fucks weren't all bad, Micah thought as he lowered his head between Isla's legs.

At least, that's what he would be telling himself until he could get a taste of Ellie.

• • •

a/n: firstly, i apologize for my absence! i was on vacation thanksgiving week and had no service until i returned, which is why i didn't wish you all for thanksgiving. on that note, happy belated thanksgiving to everyone! i hope you all had a wonderful day! once i got back home and had service, i couldn't log on because i was so bogged down with schoolwork. i haven't sleep more than 4 hours this week so i'm a little tired haha. i hoped to update this before i left for vacation but clearly that's not how things went down, haha. anyway, i hope you guys enjoyed this chapter! y'all now know the intensity of some of the content so, again, if you aren't mature enough for this, no biggie. just stop reading. i don't want to taint your innocence haha. thank you all so much for the support on this story! it really means a lot! i hope to talk to everyone soon <3 (also, i finished crooked kingdom last week and i'm crying someone help me) (also the midseason finale for how to get away with murder has me so shook and dead inside someone help me)

03 | cradle

[dedicated to because i just read her book Phantoms & Demons earlier today and my mind was actually blown to smithereens. not even exaggerating when i say that - it was that good. plus, she goes by mor and that's like one of my favoritest names ever because that's the name of a bomb af character from a bomb af book so she knows what's up]

PAPER HEARTS | 03

Ellie wasn't used to having any peace of mind - either she was in the clinic with fellow nurses shouting at her for supplies, or she was with Micah who was never short of something to talk about. There were only two, very brief, periods of time that she had to herself: her half hour shower, and her hour workout - which was also frequently interrupted by phone calls from Micah or occasional check-in's, as he liked to call it. He claimed it was to make sure she hadn't worked herself to exhaustion, but Ellie's theory was that Micah couldn't stand being by himself.

Not that she could blame him, though. When they were in the house together, only the two of them, separated from each other by a concrete wall, sometimes Ellie swore she could hear whimpers from the other side. Moans, more specifically. It was in times like those - when she imagined

Micah pleasuring himself - that she found herself diving for her laptop, manuscript already pulled up. He seemed to have any easy time jerking off to anything. Ellie, on the other hand, didn't have it very nice. It wasn't that she wouldn't give herself the opportunity at a little release - which she direly needed - but that she couldn't. While she very well knew what to do, she had no idea how to do it. She didn't know what exactly rapture was supposed to be a result of, and imagining Micah just felt wrong.

While Micah didn't have a problem going to Isla for a little fun time, as he, again, liked to call it, Ellie had a difficult time getting any kind of rise out of her boyfriend, Isaac Michaelson. The affection was there - the peppering of kisses across her forehead and the teasing touches along the palms of her hands, but there was rarely anymore than that. Ellie sometimes struggled to remember the last time he'd actually kissed her, because the quick pecks he left her with were becoming increasingly dull.

It was true that, while Micah and her were terrible in their relationships, choosing to focus on their friendship more than their potential second half, he had it better of than her. Ellie didn't struggle to push down the balloon of jealousy that swelled in her chest at the thought of that; she just feared the day the balloon would pop.

• • •

"There was only so much time she could spend yearning for the man she could never have. Standing at the crossroads of their hearts, she reached a hand out to him, but he didn't take it. He would never take it because for as long as she had loved him, he had loved someone else. His heart was packaged and shipped to one who didn't feel like she deserved it. And while the one who wanted it would never have it, she supposed she would have to come to terms with that - love was, after all, ephemeral. There was no falling in love with the beauty when she was as beastly as anything, or anyone, could get."

Ellie set her phone aside, cranking up the music and the speed on her treadmill. Running was what got her thoughts flowing - it was also what made her want to hop into bed and keep writing. Something about the idea of sweating and burning calories seemed to turn her off, but according to Isaac, exercise was going to be good for her. It was going to bring color into her cheeks, some pep into her step, and, most importantly, a significantly smaller size for jeans into her closet. Isaac stressed heavily on the last one, claiming her weight loss would be more desirable to not only him, but to herself.

She couldn't say that she disagreed with him. The only motivation Ellie had to keep working out, aside from the steady stream of thoughts crashing into each other like waves, was that by the end of it all, she'd be able to wear a tight dress without her butt bulging in the back. As surface-level as it seemed, if there was any favor Ellie could do for herself that would actually benefit her, it was losing weight.

Her breath was coming out in ragged puffs, she was beginning to see spots in her vision, when the treadmill clicked to a sudden stop. Clutching the sides, keeling over, she heaved, phlegm hanging from her lips. Her legs buckled beneath her, and Ellie came crashing to her knees, straight into a pair of waiting arms. Micah cradled her against his chest until she regained some semblance of strength. She tucked herself into his chest, hiccuping as she gasped for air - he didn't say anything when the crown of her head slammed into his jaw. He didn't say anything when she choked over the side of his arm nor when she wiped her brow on the collar of his shirt. Micah only held her tighter, only brought her closer.

"What the hell were you thinking?"

She floundered for a response. "It was just my regular workout."

"Ellie, you had it set to the fastest speed. That's not your regular workout."

He pulled her off the machine, tucked her between his thighs, dress pants brushing against her bare legs. They sat away from the lamplight, and closer to the window, clinging to each other as they were bathed in moonlight. Micah kissed her forehead, wished away the sheen of sweat. He smothered her until the embers skimming her skin caught onto him. Together, they decided, they would burn.

Everything would be done together.

"I just want to lose weight, Micah."

"Why all of a sudden? You had the same body months ago and you didn't need to lose weight.

Ellie and Micah's friendship - or whatever it was - was the paradigm of finiteness. It was a ticking time bomb, prepared to blow whenever the clock struck zero. It was a relationship built upon the foundation of a friendship. Then it turned volatile - turning into something that would, potentially, be more than what it was supposed to. Their friendship was really madness for something, or, in their case, someone. It was an obsession they had for each other. He wanted to kiss the underside of her breast, and she wanted to bite down onto his collarbone, only to lick the pain away.

"Well, now I want to lose weight - Isaac wants me to do the same."

Micah stilled behind her. "Isaac said he wanted you to lose weight?" Every word was soft, pronounced - deliberate. Ellie nodded.

"You don't think that's odd? You don't think it's odd that the man who allegedly loves every part of you is telling you to lose weight when there's no need for you to do so?"

"He's just looking out for me, Micah."

"Well, he can stop now because I've been looking after you much longer than him and I've been doing a fine job. Tell him to fuck off and mind his own business - you don't need to lose weight."

Ellie glanced up at him, her lashes barely fanning his chin. "But what if I really need to?"

"The day you need to lose weight will be the day I need to get plastic surgery. It's not going to happen. Now go shower."

• • •

a/n: long time no see, guys! so a little bit on my absence: i'm bogged down by school. whoever said senior year was a breeze lied - it's my worst year yet. i haven't had much time to write at all so for those of you looking for an update on inferno or ghost, you guys will have to wait longer. i'm so sorry about that. i hate being inactive because i'm always coming up with new ideas and i always want to share them - i just never have the time! maybe you guys caught it, maybe you didn't but ellie's a writer in the making. she's writing a story. i wonder what she could be writing? hmm. anyway, merry christmas guys! or, belated merry christmas in reality. i hope everyone had a wonderful and safe time with friends, family, and food! thank you all for the support you've shown this story - you all continue to warm my heart with every vote or comment, no matter how short so thank you for being so patient with me. you guys are the best readers in the world <3 i'm hoping to crank out another 1-2 parts for this story before my break ends so fingers crossed that i can actually pull through. have a wonderful day guys and hopefully i can talk to everyone soon in another update :)

04 | diamond

- -

[dedicated to because her book, avery, has been in my library for the longest freaking time ever and i need to get my shit together and start reading it + i adore her for supporting this story. thanks love <3]

PAPER HEARTS | 04

There was something about sugar cookies and peppermint mochas that made it seem like love was floating in the air. It was weaved into the snowflakes, transcendent and all, that dusted people's shoulders the same way it settled as constellations on their lashes. Something about shimmering ornaments and a series of twinkling, white lights brought out olive complexions, full lips, glittering smiles. Something about clusters of people huddling together to jingle bells and sing their hearts out led to fingertips brushing, connections sparking. It was then that the girl he had his arm wrapped around - the girl with blonde curls, turquoise eyes, and rose-gold lips - was no longer the only beautiful girl in the room.

There was something about the woman the crowd seemed to open up for. Her hair was silken under the golden hues of light, the sections of amber iridescent under the glare. There was something about the way she had to think through the introduction, assess its validity, before she unfurrowed her brows and allowed the corner of her lips to crinkle. Perhaps it was foreshadowing of sorts - she would be easy to love, but she wouldn't give her love away for free. Neither her smiles.

He wasn't sure how to approach her. He was just sure that when their eyes collided from across the room, he had to. If it wasn't her beauty captivating him, then it was the milk mustache embroidering her upper lip. He wanted to offer to wipe it off, or lick it away - whichever she preferred.

Her name was Isla. While he thought she was calculations, evaluations and everything in between, she was the fine line between carefree and careless - an unnatural concoction of hopeless romanticism and selflessness. She cared for everyone but herself and that's what Micah hated the most. He didn't want someone who submitted to his word complacently.

He didn't want the ashes; he wanted the flame.

When Isla offered him a sip of her hot chocolate, his gaze slipped to the girl with the turquoise eyes. He saw in her a fight that would never stop - a heart full of love but a mind wary from caution. He saw in her the fire that he dreamed of - the very fire he wished to see directed towards him. He didn't want love to come for free - he didn't want someone to expect him to be perfect; he wanted someone to make him prove he was perfect.

Her gaze met his, and the flecks of gray in her irises caught the light when the smile reached her eyes.

Her name was Ellie.

• • •

Fuzzy Friday's were a routine of relaxation for both Ellie and Micah. It was when he wore his baggiest, softest sweatpants, and she wore the fluffiest sweater. She wore the poofy hat, he wore the woolen mittens, and when they turned the temperature all the way down, together, they were a bundle of fuzz. Her chest kept him warm while his legs kept her warm. A shared coffee between their hands, and a shared bowl of popcorn between their legs, Fuzzy Friday's were ready to be kicked off with an equally fuzzy movie. While Micah always advocated an action movie with a hint of romance, a romantic movie with a hint of action always won out in the end - after all, Ellie had a fire that even Micah couldn't beat.

It was usually a half hour into the movie that Ellie would get too into it, and Micah would lose the ability to care about it. Usually, he didn't mind - he'd take the opportunity to pluck the hat off her head and run his fingers through her blonde locks, or massage her scalp. She didn't flick him away when his lips would met with the crux of her neck and collarbone - sometimes, she even leaned into his touch, flipping her hair to the side to give him more access. She tried to not mind when he'd lean over her shoulder and take a loud sip of coffee but, on an unlucky day, that would be enough to snap her out of her trance.

But tonight, for some reason, he couldn't let Ellie's mind wander.

"Ellie? I need to ask you something."

"Micah," she moaned. "Ryan Gosling is gonna be on screen in a minute!"

He snuck the remote out of his pocket and paused the movie. Ellie shifted enough to be able to turn around and shoot daggers at him, but the playfulness in her smile drifted away. She ran an icy finger over the stubble growing on his chin, up to the lip he teased between his teeth. Her worry was unspoken between them, written in the way she searched his eyes, heard the sudden hitch in his heartbeat. With the way the fun had disintegrated, a new mood settled in - one that suffocated the both of them.

He couldn't breathe.

"Is everything alright?" She pressed her forehead to his, massaged his cheeks, warmed his bare arms in the hopes of easing some of the tension out of his muscles.

He paused. "What do you think of Isla?"

"Is that what you wanted to ask me?" she asked with a giggle. "God, you had me worried for a second! But back to your question - I think Isla is wonderful. She's sweet, funny, and makes really good spaghetti. Personally, I think you should bring her over more often; I think I like her company more than yours."

"And what would you say if I told you I wanted to propose to her?"

Ellie stilled - it was hardly noticeable but she forgot to roll her thumb over the pulse in his neck. "I would say buy her the biggest, prettiest diamond ring you can find because she's worth it."

"What if I said I didn't believe you?"

She shifted again, turning her attention back to the screen. She waited to play the movie.

"Then I'd tell you to learn to."

• • •

a/n: i apologize for any typo's/grammatical errors that could be in this chapter. i was just inspired and i wanted to write as much as i could as soon as i could. so, some good news: i've finished planning paper hearts and i know exactly what's going to happen and when. i'm still working the kinks out of the ending but i think i know what i'm gonna do. the bad news: i really wanted to finish writing the story this week, but i wasn't as inspired as i thought so i couldn't finish as much as i wanted. i'm hoping to do weekly updates, probably every other week, so hopefully that'll give me a little more time to get, perhaps, a chapter done every week/every other week. thank you all for the support on this story! it really does mean the world to me! AND! if you haven't checked out ephemeral, please go do so! i'd love to know what you guys think. thank you all! i hope everyone is doing well <3

05 | touch

PAPER HEARTS | 05

warning: contains some mature content

As ephemeral as love was, it was built from years of calculation and conviction. It was made to fit the contours of the heart, mold the ridges, and stitch the fissures. It was made to adjust to the smallest of hearts, wrinkled from age or broken from misuse or dessicated from disuse; it was made to adjust to the biggest of hearts too - swelling with so much anger or hate or joy or pain that they threatened to burst. And once the love was conceived - the ability to love was cemented - it was only a matter of fierce determination to make it happen.

Love wasn't for those with paper hearts. Crumpled and thrown away, those hearts would never come back the same. They would still be hearts and they would still be paper, but their edges would be bent and their surfaces rigid. Hearts like those couldn't go through the pain necessary to come back from heartbreak. They wouldn't be able to take the heat from ironing the corners - they would capture the flame and they would cease to scream as it swallowed them entirely. They wouldn't be able to bear the weight of the world on their shoulders, flattening out the imperfections, because they would crumble to their knees. A heart like that would be no Atlas; one paperweight later, it would be torn at the seams. A paper heart, once damaged, would never resurface again. It would go into hiding, fearing any further damage - any further imperfections - to its already ruined frame. A paper heart would be fragile - but love wasn't for the fragile.

It wasn't for the weak.

Love was for those with hearts of steel - those who continued to pick at their wounds as a reminder of their suffering. Steel hearts would face the pain head on, accepting the bruises that surfaced on their skin and the occasional dents in their edges, because those hearts were unafraid. They would be willing to take the leap because love without risk, love without a game, is not love at all. Love wasn't for the weak.

It was for the strong.

It was for those willing to metamorphosize from paper to steel. It was for those willing to wait.

Ellie shut her laptop with a smile.

Love was for those willing to fight for it.

• • •

She was lying in bed in her robe, and nothing but her robe. Ellie frequently did that, normally when Micah wasn't home, but she was feeling awfully on edge. There was a pent up frustration within her that had a pulse hammering between her legs. She could attribute it to two reasons: the night before when Isaac had teased the inside of her thighs and no more, or early in the morning when she'd accidentally caught Micah slipping out of the bathroom in all his stark naked glory. Whichever it was, it had left her breathless throughout the afternoon, and impatient by the end of her shift. When she hopped into bed, hair still damp and skin still moist from the shower, Ellie didn't think twice about parting the cotton folds and letting her hand fall through.

What she was expecting was to hear Micah's snores echoing down the hall and into her bedroom. What she didn't expect was for a sleepy Micah to enter her room just as the bathrobe fell from her shoulders. When she screamed and he startled, she expected him to leave without a question while a blush ran rampant in his cheeks. What she, again, didn't expect was for him to quietly slip inside, shut the door behind him, and inch towards the edge of her bed. It didn't seem like Micah knew why he was doing what he was doing, and neither did Ellie - while she thought of covering herself, she couldn't bring her hands to move from her sides.

"Need help?" he asked, his eyes downcast. Ellie had never bothered to notice just how long his lashes were until they were fanning the balls of his cheeks. She also didn't notice the bead of sweat on his forehead or the whites of his knuckles or the straightness of his spine.

"Get out."

He started again. "You've been tense all week. If this is what's bothering you... I can help."

Ellie was quiet as he continued. "It'll be like a friend helping another friend - it doesn't have to be friends with benefits. I just help you this one night and then we never speak of it again, if that's what's holding you back."

"Why are you pushing for this so much?"

"Because I want to touch you just as badly as you want to touch yourself right now."

When he met her eyes, he held them. He held onto those turquoise eyes he loved so much because he knew that, within minutes, they were going to be fluttering shut as his command. His gaze roved over her naked body because, within seconds, it was going to bowing to the slightest touch of his fingertips. When his gaze returned to her face, to her lips, and Micah caught the slightest of nods, he knew that, from that moment on, those lips would shape to call out only his name.

She eased herself into the pillows as he neared to hover over her, knocking her legs apart with his own knees. "As you close your eyes, think about the one person you'd like to fuck the most. Doesn't have to be Isaac and you don't have to tell me - just imagine it."

A hand fisted around the waistband of his sweats, Ellie pressed her face into the pillow next to her, her lower lip caught between her teeth. Next to her, Micah propped himself up on his elbow, his free hand drawing lines along the panes of her stomach, a trail of goosebumps following in his wake. He studied her cheeks, flush with red; he studied her breasts, taught from the lukewarm water dripping from her hair; he studied her hips, bucking ever so slightly as they waited for his next set of directions.

Micah lowered his head to her chest, pressed his lips over her heart, and said, "Imagine him kneeling before you - a king brought to his knees by his queen. His head rests on your chest, relaxed, but his hands are working hard, pushing your legs apart to make room for as much as him as he can." Ellie gasped as his lips trailed up the hill of her breast, pausing to sponge a kiss on each peak, but his hand remained where it was - barely grazing her entrance.

"He waits for you to say those magic words and he knows he'll have to wait long, so he busies himself with the rest of your body. He licks the column of your neck." A lick. "He's gentle when he bites down on your nipple." A rough bite, then slight tongue to assuage the sting. "He's ravenous when he kisses his way down your torso." His lips dragged behind him, struggling to keep pace. "And when you finally say those magic words, a finger slips in."

There was no warning, no tease - he slipped in effortlessly.

"Once he's in, he's going to love how wet you are. He's going to love the effect he has on you. He's going to slip another finger in, then another, and then he's going to watch you crack before him because, like all others he's been with before, no one can resist him."

Micah fell silent after that, letting his actions speak louder than his words. Ellie's frame tilted to the side, he pressed her back harshly against his chest, letting her know that he felt the same exhilaration running through her body, electrifying her nerves. One hand palmed the underside of her breast and the other plunged deeper and deeper into her - and as all was being done, Ellie finally opened her eyes.

She finally woke up. She snagged his hand, kissed his knuckle; reached behind her to curl her fingers into his hair. The more she reacted, the harder Micah pushed for her. And when his fingers hit just the right spot - the first, then the second, then the third - she stopped breathing. She held onto him, face pale and knuckles white, and when Micah whispered, "Let go," against the shell of her ear, she finally did so.

Ellie didn't notice when his fingers disappeared, leaving her hollow on the inside. She didn't notice how moist his lips were when they kissed her goodnight nor did she notice how taut he was behind her when he slid away. All she noticed was the way he angled his body towards her as he left the room, just enough so that she could see him bring a finger to his mouth - the same finger that had been inside her seconds ago - and lick.

Lick the taste of her off his skin.

He left without a word.

• • •

a/n: i have never written anything like this before so, if it sucked, i'm so sorry i put you guys through this. please be honest and tell me whether or not this sucked so i know whether or not i should stop while i'm still ahead, haha. also! the song at the top is one that i had on repeat while writing this - i don't know why, but it made it a lot easier for me lol. anyway, thank you all for the support you've shown this story! it's really truly amazing and it really means a lot <3 in a week, i only got one more chapter down so i'm still pretty behind the schedule i had planned for myself. i still intended to update next week but then i decided against it - i'm a little swamped with midterms coming up and some subject tests around the corner so i'll just hold the update for next week and do it the week after. thank you guys for reading! your comments honestly put the biggest smile on my face. i hope everyone is doing well and i'll, hopefully, be back in action once my midterms are over!

06 | truth

PAPER HEARTS | 06

The world seemed to stop its rotation, pause on its axis, but time?

Time kept ticking on.

It followed the tick-tock of his heart and the tick-tick-tock of his breath. It ran its own rhythm even when nothing else followed; it sang its own tune when even the world around was wilted into silence. As the clock went tick-tick-tick, tap dancing alongside the rain, all the way to midnight, he felt his emotions slip-slip-slip. Sitting by himself, cloaked in nothing but darkness, there was no stopping the tears or the cries. There was no one to tell him when to stop; no one to tell him he should stop. So, without direction, he poured - he poured the rage and the grief into a bloody pile before him. He poured until his heart was as black as the midnight sky and until he felt shriveled and dead. Even then, he couldn't stop. Someone would ask him where he went wrong, and he would've said, I poured myself to ruins; I didn't know what else to do.

It was nearing the end of spring. He could make out the leaves on the trees and the flower buds on the bushes. Seasons would continue to come and go, but his father wouldn't. His father came into the world with a head of blonde hair, freckled cheeks and a wide smile, but he left with panic in his eyes and terror in his voice and there was nothing him or Micah could've done. There was nothing Micah would've done because he knew that in the second his father's hands turned clammy in his, he would've let go and he would've run. He would've had one of two choices: to lose his head without his consent or to lose it at his own hands while he was still ahead.

So when he decided on the latter, there was nothing and no one to stop him from trying to wash away the guilt. He hadn't been the one to kill his father, but he also wasn't the one who had tried to save him. Micah had been so busy trying to bury his emotions - he was so busy trying to get himself to the finish line - that he forgot all about his father. He had been so busy digging through the dirt that when he did cross the finish line, he forgot to wash his hands. They'd been dotted red; now they were doused in crimson - thick, metallic crimson. There was tequila in his system, under his fingernails, within the pockets of his pants. Wherever there was blood, there was alcohol, and when they mixed, he felt it in his bones.

He felt them grow weary. He noticed the way the bottle slipped when he lifted it to take another swig. His fingers wouldn't flex. They came crash down on shards of tinted glass. Alcohol mixed with his blood again - it burned. There was a voice in the back of his mind telling him to pick up the glass - pick up the sharpest, the shiniest, the prettiest edge he could find. There was a part of him willing his fingers to curl one last time. The voice was telling him to press that glass to his wrist, mix the alcohol and the blood, alcohol and blood, alcohol and blood. But that wasn't the only voice speaking to him.

There was a voice settling on the back of his neck. There was a body sitting behind him, in his pool of fresh tears and vomit and sweat and blood.

Slender arms were locked around his shoulder and there was a face settled on his back, pressed into the smooth section between his shoulder blades. Two lips moved against his shirt and they whispered to him - louder and louder until milk and honey were all he could hear. It was a lullaby made of echoes and trembles and hiccups - a girl's voice - and it was telling him to put the glass down. Perhaps to live one more day - live to suffer or live for happiness, he wasn't sure.

That night, there was no part of his heart that wasn't colored black but the part that Ellie managed to touch managed to beat ruby once again.

And it beat just for her.

• • •

Micah and Ellie were always home on Saturday's, which was why the two usually kept the weekends to themselves. But, to celebrate Isla's birthday in a little style, they decided to throw a party in their apartment. Micah was in charge of decorations, and Ellie was in charge of food, but the problem with the friends celebrating other people's birthday's was that they could never agree on a single decoration or food item. It was always Micah bringing up nonexistent allergies because he didn't like what Ellie offered to make, and it was always Ellie throwing a party hat at Micah's face because everything he'd set up in the last two hours was crooked.

By the time the guests were to arrive - Isaac and Isla in this case - Ellie would be sprawled across the couch, the usual slice of pizza in hand, and Micah would still be trying to get up the last of the happy birthday banners. There was one thing the two always did right though and that was the drinks. The fridge was completely empty aside from the boxes of beer shoved in, while their wine cabinet was overflowing with a single wine bottle. And what would the party be without some tequila? For the two of them, that was no party at all - rather, that was like going to church and, occasionally, confessing their sins. However, the problem with tequila that came with Micah and Ellie was that the two of them were lightweights.

Isaac always suggested pre-drinks while cutting the cake and singing happy birthday. Unfortunately, pre-drinks was all it took for either of them to get a little tipsy.

Staying true to his word, Micah mentioned nothing about their night together, but Ellie noticed the shift in his behavior. He was bolder all of a sudden, planting swift touches on the insides of her thighs whenever they sat together. His lips were always along the shell of her ear; the sweet spot behind it. He stood closer, and did so more often, but Micah was still careful. In the instances that Ellie shrugged him away, or even swerved, he stopped.

Their desire was strong; their friendship would be stronger.

Or, that's what they hoped.

When on the verge of being drunk, Micah had a tendency to go into great detail about his sexual endeavors while Ellie spilled the beans on all the sexual endeavors she wanted done to her. A little intoxication and truth or dare made for an especially deadly mix - considering Isla and Isaac were in the room. It was especially dangerous when Micah decided to pick Ellie, instead of Isaac, as his target.

"Ellie: truth or dare?"

She swayed towards Isla's shoulder. "Truth, of course."

Micah raised an eyebrow. "Remember that night from two weeks ago? Who was it you were thinking of fucking?"

Ellie lifted her bottle to her lips, making a face. "Isn't it obvious?"

When Micah shook his head, much to Isla and Isaac's dismay, Ellie said, "I was thinking of you, dumbass."

• • •

a/n: i'm back (i think)! i had finals this week but they have finally come to an end - thank goodness. i'm officially a second semester senior and i can now care about nothing! lol jk (sort of). i apologize for being absent but i'm back now and i hope that i can be more active from now on! that being said, this update is a day late but it's still an update haha. i hope you all like it! thank you so much to everyone reading and supporting this story. it honestly means the whole world to me and i cannot thank you all enough for your constant support. NOTE! i accidentally posted a coming-soon story on my account called SWEET TALKS. it's basically a cooking story (i'm obsessed with hell's kitchen) about a girl named zara who has to survive working in a kitchen run only by dudes. if that interests you, definitely check it out! thank you everyone! i hope everyone is well and i can talk to you guys in another update :) also, i'll be replying to comments as soon as i can!

07 | taunt

PAPER HEARTS | 07

She knew when there was a tempest closing in, but she never tried to protect herself from it. The clouds normally put a dapper on her mood; the winds usually ripped the umbrella out of her hand; the showers occasionally flayed her skin here or there. She had come to understand that when the forecast got bad, it was better to try to weather out the storm instead of trying to avoid it. How well she could manage to weather the storm - that made for a different story.

She didn't always have to be on the lookout for sudden hurricanes or tornados or earthquakes. There was a time, once upon a time, that she could hold the hand of whomever she wanted and still see joyous eyes. There was a day when she could hug the body of whomever she wanted and still kiss teasing lips. There was a moment when she could kiss the cheek of whomever she wanted and still return to welcoming arms. But love wasn't always smooth sailing. There was no such thing as love without fights, but sometimes she found herself asking if there could be love when there was nothing but fights.

"Why is it that you care for him more than you care for me?"

She scoffed. "That's not the case and you know it."

But he didn't know it, and, unfortunately, neither did she. The longer she was in one relationship, the more she seemed the devoted to another. The less faithful she appeared, the angrier he became. There were times when the tempest was survivable but more often than not, neither of them came out unscathed.

The clouds set in place as the lights dimmed; the sudden flash of his palms usually smacked her own out of the way whenever they shot up to shield her face; a downpour of glass cleaved through her ear, or collar, or forearm.

At the end of the storm, when his fists were just short of her face and his breath was cold on her neck and his body was pressed uncomfortably close to hers, there was always a threat looming over her hunched shoulders.

The next time something like this happens, the glass won't be the only thing leaving this apartment broken.

• • •

As she kicked the key out from underneath the carpet, Ellie couldn't help but pray. Words formed on her lips but she couldn't manage the voice to articulate her thoughts - please be in a good mood; please don't blow up; please be a good boyfriend. But she sensed a storm in the distance. Outside, the sky was fuzzy, smudged with shades of grey. The ground shook beneath her; she felt the thunder thrum through her bones. Ellie knew that the minute she opened her mouth to apologize to Isaac, the rain was going to fall. It was going to pitter on the balcony, patter against kitchen window.

The crackle of water and the howl of wind was going to drown out the tremble in her voice.

When her head peeked past the door, she noticed the glass of whiskey in Isaac's hand. It took all the strength in her to keep from closing the door and running the other way.

"Took you long enough to get back to me," he said, sipping at his drink.

"I've been busy," she started, lamely.

"Busy with work or busy fucking Micah?"

Cue the lightning.

There was a time in her life when Isaac trusted her. Perhaps not Micah, but he trusted her word and her self-control. It wasn't unusual for him to ask what she'd done with Micah - especially on days they spent together - but he never minded her brutal honesty when it came to her best friend. He respected them as people and he tried to respect their relationship as best as he could. Ellie, however, didn't blame Isaac for his misconstrued theories and constant doubt. Sometimes, when she tried to imagine herself in his shoes, she experienced similar feelings of suspicions.

It was Micah who was reassuring her that they were friends and nothing more. It was him giving her weekly lectures about how best friends could be close to each other without having to be anymore. In truth, he wasn't convincing anyone - more than anything, he spoke to make himself feel better. Both Ellie and Micah knew that they weren't just friends. People who were, quite literally, only friends didn't ogle each other or shamelessly kiss each other's necks or cuddle at any given opportunity. They certainly didn't touch each other whenever they felt like it. And, unfortunately, since she couldn't convince herself that her and Micah were just friends, it was unlikely she was going to be able to convince Isaac of the same thing.

"Isaac, I was drunk. I didn't know what I was saying."

"I'm just confused as to why you would say his name over mine? It's not like I wasn't in the room with you."

Although surviving the hurricane was near impossible, Ellie had discovered a way to prolong the calm before the storm. Shutting the door behind her, the closed the distance between her and a seated Micah. The leather of the couch cushioned her knees on both sides of him and she rested her weight on his thighs, but Isaac made no move to support her. One arm remained limp at his side while the other clung to his drink. Refusing to make eye contact, he turned his head to manage a sip.

"Ellie, I don't want you touching me."

She caressed his cheek. "Look me in the eyes and tell me you mean that."

"Fine." A hand shot out and grappled onto her chin, fingers digging into her cheeks.

"Ellie Harte, I don't want you to fucking touch me because I don't know where those hands of yours have been. For all I know and care, they could've been all over Micah's body before you came to my place. You can tell me whatever you want, but nothing you say will make me trust you because, as far as I know, when we're not together, all you're thinking about is fucking Micah. Sometimes I have to ask myself why I'm still dating you despite, in spite, of all this.

She shook away his grip; leaned away from his touch. Ellie was almost on her feet. "Yeah? If you feel that way, why are you still dating me?"

"Because I feel bad for you, Ellie! If I don't date you, who the hell will? No one wants used goods - you and Micah are a package deal. No guy is going to want to put up with the insecurity that his girlfriend is potentially fuck- ing another guy behind his back! You're beautiful, babe - I will never deny that - but you're also not what a guy wants. Your face, your intelligence, and your personality will never be able to make up for your body. You're thinking I'm wrong, aren't you? That if you broke up with me right now and went running to Micah, he'd forget about Isla and sweep you off your feet? Why don't you go ask him yourself, Ellie? Go ask Micah if he'd date you."

But Ellie would never ask him that; it didn't matter how much Isaac taunted her.

She wouldn't ask him because when she herself felt that she was unworthy of his love, how was she going to convince him otherwise?

• • •

a/n: i thought i'd update a little early today because GUESS WHAT GUYS?! i got into the university of michigan - the college of my dreams! throwback to december when i was deferred and was the ultimate mess haha. i'm honestly so happy because it was so unexpected and i was actually genuinely expecting to be rejected so i'm literally over the moon right now, haha. and, now that i'm officially a second semester senior (now that i'm accepted, i can breathe lol) paper hearts will definitely be finished (at least the writing). i've finally been able to get back to writing and i'm currently working on the 9th chapter. my projection is that this story have around 16 chapters? that's just an estimate though. thank you all so much for reading this story and being so patient with it! i'm very on and off wattpad and i apologize for that - i can only hope to be more active from now on though! i hope to talk to everyone soon - perhaps in an another update? let's see if i can update weekly, haha. again, thank you all so much and i hope you enjoyed!

08 | chicken

[dedicated to because she's such a wonderful trailer maker and she's been such a great friend and mentor to me these past few weeks i've had the opportunity to get to know her. she's an absolute sweetheart and i adore with her all my heart <3]

PAPER HEARTS | 08

warning: contains some mature content

Isla was a firm believer in her first love being her last and only love, which was why she had been so intent on Micah accompanying her to her baby sister's marriage in London. While Micah hadn't been fond of the idea of leaving his succulent alone in Ellie's hands, he also hadn't been willing to pass up some quality time with Isla. Undoubtedly, the relationships he had with both girls had their benefits. While with Isla it was a constant sweet, slow, and sultry, with Ellie it was a fair balance between fire and ash. One relationship was a fairy tale; the other was an adventure.

Following four cups of coffee at the Boston airport, both Micah and Isla were wide awake - and very, very aroused, for whatever reason. It was an hour into the flight when the windows were shut and the lights were switched off dimmed. Another hour passed before the elderly woman besides Isla dozed off. Only after he was sure everyone in their section of the flight was asleep did Micah slip his hand under Isla's blanket and into the waistband of her sweats. She neither looked at him when he gazed at her nor did she flinch when his ice-cold hand dipped into her core. Micah wasn't happy with her response.

He leaned in close enough for the scruff on his cheeks to brush against hers. Isla blinked. When he pulled out one earplug with his tongue, catching it between his teeth, she smacked his free hand tiptoeing towards her breasts.

"I thought you said you wanted me," he murmured in her ear.

"That was before I started watching a movie," she hissed.

"Bullshit."

When the pad of his thumb began to massage her and a second finger begin to writhe on the inside, Isla managed to tear her gaze away from the miniature screen. Her breath came out in ragged puffs as she pressed her forehead painfully close to Micah's. "Say something to me," she moaned, albeit softly.

The armrest pushed up, Micah scooted closer until she was practically in his lap. When her eyes fluttered shut, he licked up the column of her neck before pausing at her lips. "You wanna know what I'm going to do to you once we get to the hotel room?"

A pause.

"We aren't going to make it to the bedroom. I'm going to take you in the kitchen, or the couch - whichever is the closest. Maybe even the floor if I have to. Once I've got you splayed out for me, those sweats are going. Your panties too. My hands running from your ankles to your knees, I'm going to have you begging before I push your legs wide open for me. I want to see you touching yourself as I kiss your inner thigh and then the junction of your hips before I taste you. And Isla? You're gonna be the only thing I eat all night.

"I want you to feel my tongue against you, inside you. When I capture you between my lips, maybe even my teeth, I'm gonna have you screaming my name loud enough for arriving guests to hear you. Maybe your sister will even hear us, yeah? When my fingers dig into your hips, I want you to groan; when I pull your hips closer to me, you're gonna start bucking. Don't rush me, Isla - I'm not done dining until I say I'm done."

Sometime in the middle of his tale, Micah's voice had turned ragged and his breath had become labored. It was only when he paused his narrative that he comprehended that Isla's hand was, indeed, down his pants. He couldn't remember when her hand slipped in or when she'd started pumping him, but he was coming close. Her fingertips were already slick as they continued to run up the length of him.

"I'm almost there," she said.

"It doesn't matter what it is - whatever piece of furniture is closest to us, I'm going to have you bent over it until your legs give out."

When release came barreling through Isla, Micah followed suit. Their lips followed the same rhythm and their hands were in sync, but their heads had not yet caught up to each other.

While Isla did actually moan his name, Micah groaned the forbidden word: "Ellie."

• • •

The best part about hanging out at Isla's apartment was when, at quarter to nine, Micah and her crowded into her miniature kitchen to cook up whatever her inner chef decided it wanted that night. The best part about cooking together was that, no matter how specific the recipe, they somehow made every argument about how much salt and pepper to add or whether to use chicken or pork, end with a food fight. The best part about having a food fight with each other was that, in spite of the spices dotting the walls, it always ended with the two having sex. The worst part about having sex while cooking, however, was that they always managed to set off the smoke detector.

Too hungry to wait for takeout, the two would always end up eating the burnt chicken, or pork.

But cooking with Isla was only fun when she was in a good mood, and when she dodged the kiss he intended to plant on her cheek, he knew he wasn't going to be getting anything from her that night. It was usually Micah who angered her more than her upsetting him, and understandably so. While Isla's affections were directed solely towards him, his affections were divided between two. Isla had defined a line for Micah and Ellie's friendship - she was kind in that sense. Patient, as well. However, boundaries meant nothing to Micah when his girlfriend wasn't around and he found it more and more difficult to abide to her wishes.

On the occasion that they would fight, Micah always asked her why she refused to break up with him if he made her so upset. Isla's answer was always the same: she knew he still loved her. His feelings for Ellie may have been growing like a wildfire, but his relationship with Isla continued to be a slow, slow burn. It had its ups and downs; it could be leisure and boring; it was calm and quiet. But there was one prime difference between the two relationships.

A wildfire is quick. The sparks - the initial meeting - start the flame. The flame grows rapidly - built upon a single conversation, or physical interaction, or attraction - until it's taking down its surroundings. The fire spreads as the relationship quickens - fewer emotional connections and more physical action - until it burns everything in its wake. It burns until there's nothing left for it to burn. Until no aspect of the relationship can catch up to the speed at which it progresses. Its fire dies out first, then its heart.

But for something to slowly burn - the relationship is built on development. The spark may be struck and it may catch the tinder, but it cannot grow until it's nurtured. The gap of time is filled with talks and teases, dates and kisses until the becoming of the flame. Until the attraction finally becomes definite. In the time that the fire remains alight, it may swell. The relationship may become as physical as it is emotional. It may shrink; the relationship may become an amalgamation of arguments and, in rare cases, distrust. However, the fire always returns to its original size. It continues to burn all because, when something can grow at its own pace, it's easy to put in the effort to tend to it - care for it.

"Do you want to know why Ellie said my name the other day?"

Isla shook her head. "What you and Ellie do together is not of my concern. What your friendship is built upon should be kept a secret - the same way what we do in our relationship is kept private."

Micah wrapped an arm around her naked waist, resting his chin on her shoulder as she pushed the chicken this way and that. He didn't have the heart to grab her wrist and tell her that the recipe called for the chicken to just sit. "I know you don't believe that. Let me explain what happened, Isla."

While Isla tried to shrug him off, and momentarily succeeded, Micah returned the same position, holding on tighter. But he didn't dare push her.

"Micah, I appreciate you wanting to tell me; I respect that. But I really don't wanna know because I know that whatever you're going to tell me is going to hurt. A lot. Just drop the topic and we'll move on from it."

There were a couple of things Micah had learned about Isla since they had started dating. One realization was that whenever Isla tried to lie, the tips of her ears turned a bright pink and her leg would start to bounce, whether or not she was standing.

Her ears were scarlet.

"Baby, it's bothering you. If you're not gonna let me explain myself, at least give me the chance to make things better? Tell me what I need to do to fix this."

She dropped the spatula and turned the heat on the stovetop completely off. While the chicken still seemed a little pink, she dumped it all into a mixing bowl and turned to face him. Her eyes were swollen and puffy, red lining her irises. "If I asked you to move in with me - if I told you that would be the only way to fix this, would you do it?"

"She's my best friend, Isla."

Isla smiled, but when it didn't quite reach her eyes, Micah knew he'd the said the wrong thing. He dropped his gaze when she laid a warm palm flat against his cheek. "I know she is - that's why I didn't want to ask. I knew you wouldn't be able to do it."

• • •

a/n: note: the clip at the top is the music that really helped me write this chapter; i have no idea why lol. i'm late on an update. i know. i've just been uninspired to do anything, and it doesn't help that my laptop crashed. luckily, i work on google drive and not word so i didn't lose anything in the writing aspect. can't say the same for everything else though, haha. also, i apologize for any grammatical errors beforehand - i didn't necessarily proofread this chapter! while i did have mid-winter break this week, i didn't get any writing done, unfortunately. a friend of mine has been hounding me to watch game of thrones and while i promised her i'd start watching during spring break, i started a little early and ngl, i'm lowkey kind of obsessed. i mean, in 72 hours, 32 of them were spent watching game of thrones. i started monday with 1x01 and by wednesday night, i was 4x03 so - my binging at it's finest haha. thank you all for reading this! i know i'm absolutely horrible at updating and i'm sorry about that! however, everyone's support means the absolute world to me and i cannot thank you all enough for it <3

09 | coral

- -

[dedicated to because she actually has such a good taste in books (and tv shows tbh) and she's recommended some amazing books to me (some of which i've actually read already and loved to death). plus, she's just such a fun, kind, lovable girl that i always have to dedicate a chapter to her. that's how much she means to me <3]

PAPER HEARTS | 09

warning: contains some mature content

His hair was silken under the palms of her hands, curling seamlessly around each fingertip she had threaded into his roots. Hazel eyes alight like the fire crackling next to their nearly-naked bodies, he didn't try to mask the shadow crossing his features as his head descended past her jawline. His lips, wet and swollen when they ran across her own, sponged a brief kiss along the underside of her breast before painting their way downwards. And they painted like an artist whose last breath depended on his masterpiece. His tongue dipped and flicked and sucked and ravaged.

He dotted her body with hues of indigo and coral and wine and cream; his kisses were messy and erratic and speckled her just barely. Wherever his tongue and lower lip dragged across the panes of smooth skin were brushstrokes of lavender and teal and burgundy. As his teeth nipped, she witnessed a streak of crimson embroider the raised flesh. However, she didn't care that her breasts were painted lilac or her navel sapphire or her lips scarlet; she only cared that, at the apex of her hips, he was painting her with every color he knew. With each stroke of his tongue, she witnessed that masterpiece she was meant to be actually come to be.

His hands, roaming her body, smudged the paints. They spread one one way, and mixed another another way. Fragmented fractals penciled into her skin while textures dug into her sides. Perhaps choosing to make love on the newly replaced carpet in the barely furnished living room in the hardly empty cabin was not their best idea, but he was persuasive. His nephews were fast asleep, their snores emanating from the bedroom through the cracked door. When a moan started to slip past her, his messy hand pursed her lips shut - muffled her voice until it no longer existed.

But the artist was not satisfied with painting only the outside; he wanted his paints to bleed through the canvas. His lips halted the voice in her throat, swallowing the scream before she could breathe life into it. When she clung to him, locking her ankles around his waist and pressing her body flush against his, the paints smeared. The designs disappeared between them, but neither of them cared. His artwork was almost finished. Four strokes later - he was counting - she would be all his, inside and out. Her heart would beat his blood, her lungs would breathe his air, and her lips would only know his name.

He wanted to present his jewel to the world - display her for the whole world to see. His name signed in the corner, he wanted lingering eyes to know she was his, and his only. But as her breathing evened, he knew his showcase would have to wait. The two of them wrapped in a quilt, he feathered kisses along her brow and cheek until her chest rose and fell in the slightest. Until the barest breath teased his chest when it blew past parted lips. A sheen of sweat was glistening along her hairline.

When she woke up the next morning as the sun was rising over the horizon, she jolted to the empty space next to her. In its place was a note reading, Went out to grab some groceries. Make sure you're dressed before the kiddos wake up - can't have them making moves on my beautiful, naked girlfriend. Clothes hidden underneath the quilt and her body draped conservatively, she made her way to the master bedroom - to the full length vanity mirror tucked into the corner of the bathroom. While she had been too tired to examine the art he had made of her the night before, there was no chance she could forget to see it. However, when the heavy material fell from her shoulders, she wished she had washed the colors away.

Expecting a bouquet of fresh daisies, tulips, and roses haphazardly thrown together to form a technicolor piece, her hand came to her mouth as she took in the monochromatic despondence of the wilted garden. In mixing colors together - some that belonged, most that didn't - and letting the creation sit overnight, he had ruined her.

Emerging from his arms decorated as the bleakest night sky, she was the Queen to a Dark King. But she also wasn't. Underlying her glossed exterior was a beating heart full of love and life. As she mulled over what he had made of her, she realized that she should've known what he would try to turn her into. As it would be for any other King who ruled only darkness, his favorite color was black. Black, in turn, was the absence of color and he - Isaac - was the absence of a human.

• • •

Her Friday afternoons were spent lounging on the couch, her laptop resting on her stomach and a plate of lettuce wraps waiting for her on the coffee table. There was no better time than lunchtime to get her thoughts flowing - no noise, no music, and especially no Micah.

Micah himself was only useful whenever she was trying to get some romance done. In his absence, she managed to finish everything else - both plot and character development. According to publishers, if she was ever going to get the book into stores, she was going to have cut down on the heat and build on the story arch. They claimed that no one was willing to read about a strong female character loving, and potentially banging, two men at once - much to the unawareness of the other interest. On the contrary, Ellie believed that, while her story was nothing like editors and publishers made it to be, if people could enjoy Fifty Shades of Grey, they could enjoy her work.

Nonetheless, she agreed to change it.

Calla Ardelene was a warrior in some sense. A slum rat from a young age, all she knew to do was fight, steal, and survive. On the occasion, she could also have a good time at the very back of the market with the boy with the run for lust tattooed over his heart. However, just as Calla was in love with one man, she was in love with a shadow - a creature hidden in the depths of the forest watching her every move. The man with the tattoo knew how to make her scream his name and walk funny for the next day or two. But the man of the shadows knew how to bring something rare out of her - a smile. He knew how to make her feel like she was just as privileged as those of the kingdom. One touch was fleeting like the tickle of a feather, while the other was hot like the ember struck by a match.

One love was like Isaac's - a mix of adventures and expensive treats and dangerous glass showers. The other was like Micah's - all inside jokes and unnerving teases and childish fun.

Ellie shoved a lettuce wrap into her mouth just as the doorbell rang. Expecting it to be Micah coming home for his lunch break, she didn't bother to try to lick the sriracha stain off her shirt or put on a pair of pants to hide her unshaven legs. It was a terrible decision given Isla was standing on the opposite side of the door, prim and proper as usual with his manicured hands and dazzling smile. Isla frowned, greeting her with a mumble as she stepped to the side. It wasn't that Ellie disliked Isla; she disliked the perfection.

She sometimes wondered what would've happened if she had been, to some arbitrary extent, as perfect as Isla. Perhaps then Micah would've picked her and neither Isla nor Isaac would've existed anywhere in their story line.

Their routine was easy, the same way Ellie's was with Micah. Ellie offered lunch; Isla politely declined, offering up some of her own lunch instead. Isla asked to read some of Ellie's manuscript; Ellie allowed her to read the latest, finished chapter. Isla asked about Ellie's job, Ellie asked about Isla's job, and both always laughed at mundanity of their lives.

Isla was an simple person to get along with. Talkative, forgiving, and kind, she made Ellie feel as if she was talking to Micah. They were perfect for each other in that sense; however, they differed in terms of thinking. Isla knew what she wanted at all times but Micah often required some form of convincing.

"So I'm going to be completely honest with you and tell you that there's an ulterior motive to my visit today - aside from it being a month since I last came for lunch," Isla laughed.

"Should I be worried?" Ellie asked, scrunching her nose.

"Maybe? I mean, I came to talk to you about Micah. He told me about what you two did together some weeks ago."

The breath halted in Ellie's lungs, color rushing into her pale cheeks. She braced herself with the fear that Isla would yell at her - perhaps even hit her if she was feeling that passionate. But when she received no blow, Ellie cast Isla a quizzical look, making a face as Isla's teasing smile. "You're not upset?"

Isla nudged her shoulder. "I'm more upset by the fact that you'd think I'd be upset. Come on, Ellie! You know me - I wasn't even mad the ex-boyfriend who kicked me out of my own apartment."

That was, in fact, true.

She continued. "It's an awkward position to be, of course. Realizing my boyfriend is in love with another girl just as much as he's in love with me - if not more - is not something I thought I'd have to deal with, but here I am. And funny enough, I'm not angered by it at all. But, I mean, at the end of the day, if there's anyone I'd want Micah to be with - someone I knew could make him happy - it would be you. And I guess I really just came here to tell you that I'm alright with all of this. I know you love him, and I know he's got some sort of feelings for you. I know it would be wrong of me to try and break your guys's friendship when the feelings you two have for each other are so real."

"What are you trying say?"

"I think I'm trying to say that, no matter who he picks at the end of the day, I'll be happy with it just as long as he's happy. I hope you can say the same?"

Ellie took a shaky breath, but managed a small smile. "So, in a hypothetical situation, if Micah picked me, what would you do?"

Isla feigned contemplation before answering with a giggle. "Uh, the only other thing to do: I'd steal Isaac."

"You don't want to do that."

"Come on! Why not? I should be able to have a chance with your boyfriend if Micah takes you off the market!"

Ellie thought of her next words very carefully, hoping to not make her relationship too explicit while still giving Isla a hint as to what it had managed to become. He's violent. He's controlling. He'd use your kind heart in his favor; he'll make you believe his mistakes are yours. He'll hit you. He'll treat you like the dirt on the bottom of his shoes. He'll push you away and expect you to come running back each time. He'll kill you if you don't.

Without any emotion in her voice, without any expression on her face, Ellie whispered, "He's just not the person everyone thinks he is."

• • •

a/n: i apologize for missing the update yesterday (and if there are any grammatical errors in this)! i decided to go to a dance competition with my friends - desi tashan - with my friends last minute. if any of you guys ever have any kind of dance competition anywhere near you, go. they're honestly so fun. aside from the amazing dancing, there are some seriously hot guys there (it's a plus if they can dance) (excuse me i'm the ultimate hoe at heart). i laughed so much, screamed so loud, and found the love of my life. last night was a night well spent. the competition went until 11, and then i was out shopping for a prom dress all day today. however, i finally found a dress!! thank the lords!! so, as a celebration, i'm here with this longer-than-usual update but i hope you guys like it! while isla isn't as much of a main character, she's a very important part of micah's life and even if you guys don't like her as much as ellie, i hope she grows on you in some sense. thank you all for the constant love you guys give this story. it means so so much to me <3

10 | belle

[dedicated to because i saw that she added this story to her reading list and literally almost died in my bed. plus, sam & marley, which i read a long, long time ago (maybe when this account had 50 followers?) was one of my absolute favorite books on this site. now she's got a new story out called above the clouds and i'm dying guys - i'm literally dying to read this book because her writing does wonders on you]

PAPER HEARTS | 10

The first snowflakes on winter were sifted onto the ground as they made their way out of the restaurant and to the hotel across the street. Hints of the night sky bled over the orange-yellow hue of light and the winter breeze snaked into their coats. The shivers rippled along her spine and gooseflesh spotted her naked arms. A gasp tore at her lips when the pads of her fingertips pressed against the palms of his gloved hands. He looked down at her with a knowing look as if to say, I told you it was cold outside. He was right - he had chastised her when she started to leave their apartment in nothing but a dress and a woolen fleece. If it hadn't been for the jacket he'd forced around her shoulders, he would've been waiting an extra hour to reveal his birthday present for her because she'd be thawing before the hotel fireplace.

Mitchell Matthews, Micah's older brother, always arrived in town the week of Christmas to celebrate the eve with Ellie, the day of with his girlfriend, and the day after with Micah. Well - Mitchell didn't necessarily spend Christmas Eve with Ellie, but he made arrangements for Ellie and Micah to waste the day together. The specialty of Christmas day was that Ellie's birthday would the day before and Micah's would be the day after. The specialty of Mitchell's arrival was that with the thousands of dollars he always showed up with, he had plenty of money to go around.

While most birthday celebrations were experienced through lavish presents, Mitchell thought to help Micah make Ellie's twenty-second birthday especially memorable. Micah had spent a lot of time thinking before he approached his brother - he needed a practical, viable reason for wanting to borrow Mitchell's penthouse suite for the night. He knew that if he told his older brother that he was trying to impress Ellie by creating her best daydream, the teases would never end. Or worse - Mitchell would try to get involved and act as Micah's wingman.

It was around his half birthday that Micah began to feel some inkling of attraction towards Ellie and her ways. It was childish of him to accept his emotions as easily as he did, considering Ellie was beginning to show some interest in the McDreamy at the hospital, but that didn't stop Micah from trying. It was his inner friend, as well as his suppressed boyfriend, that was planning Ellie's birthday - not that she knew, of course. A new pendant for her charm bracelet and lunch (anything but dinner was a little unorthodox for Ellie) were the usual; it was everything following that made Ellie gush to her friends about her birthday for the next year.

For her nineteenth, he'd driven her to the his lakeside cabin in Michigan's upper peninsula. For her twentieth, Mitchell had helped him save up enough money to get him and Ellie two tickets to Disneyland; he secretly kept a printed picture of her and Merida in his wallet because he'd never seen anyone look as beautiful, or as happy, around a Disney character.

Much to his chagrin, Ellie paid Mitchell back before the new year. Her twenty-first, although it was no vacation, was the first celebration to bring tears to her eyes. He'd bought her diamond earrings which, from that day on, she wore to every party, dinner, or potluck, whether or not the two went together.

Micah intended to up the ante for her twenty-second.

He was going to try to recreate her senior prom.

The bronze accents of the walls, the silver of the lights and the hanging bluebells in the suite made it seem like a ballroom fresh out of her favorite Disney movie. Micah was no beast, though he had intended to ask Mitchell to rough him up a little in order to look like one. But Ellie, in her tulle periwinkle and gold gown, looked like a true Belle - an actual beauty to a wannabe beast.

After the last three years of pampering, hardly anything fazed Ellie - extravagant surprises were a custom at that point in their friendship. Each birthday made her adore Micah a little more, but when he led her onto the balcony of the suite that night, all she could think about was being in love with a man like him. Micah was undoubtedly handsome, but he was also kind and funny and smart in his own way and, in some sense, that made him far more attractive than he truly was. As he asked her if she could feel the love tonight, his humming echoing in her ear, she dared to glance up at his face, the soft features highlighted under the starry night sky. His hands on her waist, her arms wrapped around his neck and her head on his shoulder, Ellie dared to imagine a future.

She imagined what it would be like to kiss his cheeks, then his lips. She imagined wondering if he truly tasted like raspberries the same way he smelt of them. She smiled at the thought of waking up next to his naked body every morning and enjoying a platter of pancakes after a shared shower. She pictured a diamond ring on her finger to match her earrings and a honeymoon to the Caribbean. Ellie envisioned a little Theo and Abel in her arms as Micah kissed her forehead.

Most importantly, she could imagine a future - one that had seemed fuzzy until that moment.

"What are you thinking about?" Micah asked with a smile. She could tell he was disappointed he couldn't look like the beast, but Ellie was glad he didn't. She thought the look of a prince suited him much better.

"I was just thinking about what a future with you would look like," she answered honestly.

"Yeah? What did it look like? Promising, I'd hope."

She returned that loving smile of his. "It was better than any future I could ask for."

• • •

Micah was changing things up for Ellie's twenty-fourth and he wasn't happy about it. For whatever reason, he didn't think that a sixth charm bracelet, movie, and dinner would suffice, but that was likely because he was getting too used to having Mitchell's money to spend. Unfortunately, Mitchell and his girlfriend Alice were going to be in Paris for the Christmas and New Year's, so Micah wasn't going to be having any fancy hotel rooms or vacation tickets to gift Ellie with. It wasn't that he couldn't afford riches; it was just that his family looked down on his extravagance. He'd learned to reign in his expensive taste at a young age, only daring to spend when he was given the permission or the money to do so.

Ellie, once again, could tell there was something off about his behavior. It was as if she had a sixth sense dedicated to knowing when he was disappointed himself. She reached across their dinner table, lacing their fingers together, knocking aside his bowl of red curry noodles.

"How'd you know I wanted to watch the live-action Beauty and the Beast anyway?" she questioned. "I never told you."

He shrugged. "I'm your best friend. It's my duty to know these kind of things."

"Well, you must be the greatest best friend in the world for knowing that because that was, hands down, the best birthday present you've given me over the years. Truly."

Though he seemed reluctant, Micah perked just barely. "Really?" he asked, hopeful.

She nodded vigorously, making a scene to leap onto the table. Micah witnessed a twenty-four year old woman regress back to a seven year old watching the classic Beauty and the Beast for the very first time. As she made her way about the table, stepping here and stepping there, Micah picked up the platters of food, setting them on the chairs beside him but never taking his eyes off of her. He sat in a stunned silence as she waved to him, the walls, the kitchen, and the patio saying, "Bonjour!" He made a mistake of resting his elbows on the table, having been so entranced in his performance, that when she thrust her hands into the air welcoming him to be her guest, she almost kicked him in the face. Micah sat back with an amused laugh when she puffed out her chest and pointed her fork at him, claiming she was Gaston.

Ellie waltzed about the table, humming the title song, pretending the loose hem of her shirt was her beast, and there was something enchanting about her performance. She was no theater girl nor was she a dancer, but in those few moments, she was both. She was an artist with her expressions, each smile drizzled sparsely and each tear shed carefully. Her movements were fluid and deliberate, powerful as she transformed into Gaston, gentle as she became Belle, and even more so as the Beast entered the scene. Micah wondered if he could get her into acting if her writing career didn't take off like he hoped. But if there was anything more difficult than getting Ellie to accept her body for what it was, it was getting Ellie to come out of her shell.

So lost in his thoughts, Micah didn't realize Ellie had stopped her performance to kneel before him until her fingers were caressing his cheeks. "Would you help for the last act?"

Standing up, Ellie extended a hand to Micah but he was hesitant to take it. "I don't think our table will be able to handle this much weight."

"Believe me," she giggled, pulling him up anyway. "This table has faced far worse than the two of us standing on it."

Although he didn't dwell on the statement, Micah made a mental note to disinfect the table in case Ellie might have forgotten.

"Now don't tell me I'm Gaston, Ellie. I don't like the idea of being pushed off the table."

She shook her head. "I already finished that part of the movie, buddy. Beast has just transformed back into Prince Adam."

Oh.

"So, what happens in the last act?"

She wasn't meeting his gaze when her hands slid up the creases in his shirt. "You know what happens."

"You'll have to remind me."

So Ellie, with her sideswept hair, rouge lips, and baby blue eyes, stood one step closer to him. Their gazes never broke away nor did their hands ever part. When she stood on her toes, Micah met her halfway. The stubble along his jawline was rough against her cheeks but when she ran her hands along the sides of his face, the touch just barely there, the soft moan that slipped past his lips did indescribable things to her. She felt his touches on her arms, her legs, her stomach, and she felt them within. There was a knot developing in her gut as his arm snaked around her waist and pulled her closer.

The kiss was slow. The kiss was calculated. Every move of his lips was done with the intent to brush hers. Each stroke of his tongue was intended to set her on fire just a little more. When he sucked her lower lip into his mouth and nibbled, he did so knowing he would, then, be the only thing on her mind.

"Beauty," he whispered ever so softly, breaking away to press a kiss to her forehead.

Then, the table broke.

"I told you it wouldn't make it," Micah said, pushing her hair aside.

"Well, it looks like we'll have to redo that last scene then."

Neither objected.

• • •

a/n: please let me know if there are any errors in this! i didn't have a chance to proof read before updating because i wanted to get this out there - i didn't want to miss two updates in a row haha. i did consider it though. i don't know what it was about this chapter but it was, by far, the most difficult chapter of me to write. i deleted 3 pages worth of writing almost 4 times because it was complete trash, haha. i didn't know what would help me finish this chapter until i went and watched the beauty and the beast live-action yesterday and holy shit guys!!!!! it was so good! i only watched the classic version about a month ago and i loved that but for me, the live action nailed it. the new music (please please check out evermore by dan stevens it's fucking stunning), the added storylines, the characters, the acting - everything was so marvelous! y'all have to watch it. even if you're not into the story, it's just a treat for the eyes. it's so aesthetic. i wrote all this last night + this morning so i'm still experiencing a hangover from the experience. i'm totally ok with that haha. ALSO! the dress at the top is the one ellie was described to be wearing at the beginning of the chapter, and it's also my prom dress. what do you guys think of it? thank you all for reading this story! it'll likely be my first completed story and i'm so excited! it means the world that you guys continue to read and support it and i couldn't thank you guys enough <3

11 | slice

[dedicated to because i've read almost all of her stories (Z, not dun yet,
  and hot line) and i've loved all of them. she's the short story queen. plus,
her latest story - just my type - is so addictive i absolutely adore it <3]

PAPER HEARTS | 11

It was tradition that on New Year's Eve, Isaac would take it upon himself to throw the annual 'Bowman Bash', a poorly constructed potluck complete with a play area for the children, obnoxious music for the teenagers, and a restricted tequila station for the adults. It was the only day of the year where the neighbors pretended they liked each other. Every other day was spent popping the car tires of the person who dared to park on the already narrow street. It was the one day where people tried to make small talk with each other because if not, they had no chance of getting their hands on any food, even if they were the ones to bring it.

God forbid they had to walk back to their house which was, at most, a twenty minute walk from Isaac's backyard because they would obviously starve to death by then. People were more willing to talk to their alleged 'sworn enemies' over walking back to their houses to enjoy a perfectly good frozen dinner. The narrowed eyes and pained smiles may as well have shown that the only thing stronger than our dislike for each other was our stubbornness to stay put.

Physical exercise was a big no-no.

Clusters of complaints echoed through households usually a week before the actual event - most were about my Isaac's inability to mix drinks which was, in fact, true - yet attendance was always bountiful. While most people wore their reluctance on their sleeves as they strolled through our paint-ridden fence, emotions tended to transform barely an hour into the party.

Every party had that one person where, when they walked in, a solemn hush would fall over the crowd. People stopped their chewing, drinks hovered mid-air and bodies made way. It was like when they walked into the room, the clouds parted and the sun came out for the first time in years. Voices, barely a whisper, surfaced in cliques, passing a message on from body to body: the party had officially started. In Isaac's neighborhood, the acclaimed role went to Ellie and Micah.

Usually walking into the party together, arm in arm, the two looked like a match made in heaven, clad almost all in white. Micah would fix his black bowtie and Ellie would tuck a curled lock of hair behind her ear. It was not that Isaac's party had a dress code; the two just liked to be the center of attention. Micah, always without a date because Isla spent the holidays with her family, carried Ellie on his arm since her own date was the host of the party. However, since Isaac never seemed to have time for anything but formalities, the two never quite left each other's side. Looking ethereal in each other's arms, Micah's blush pink lips complimenting her green-blue eyes, they danced the night away, toasted to a brilliant new year, and drank the morning away.

Micah always found a ride home, since he was always too drunk to drive back, but Ellie stayed the rest of the night at Isaac's. In her drunken state, it was a dream to be transferred from the arms of one beautiful man into the arms of another, and Isaac wasn't too shabby himself. Unlike Micah, Isaac's usual garb was all black, save for the white handkerchief peeking out of his breast pocket. Once the guests were all gone for the night, despite the mess made of his home, Isaac always found the time to get piss-drunk and join Ellie in bed.

But right after she turned twenty-one, for the first time, Isaac didn't follow routine.

Ellie hadn't realized Isaac had been watching when Micah had attached a new charm - a clover - to her bracelet. Even if she had noticed, she didn't think he would've cared about Micah giving her a belated present for his birthday. She didn't think he would've cared even when she gave Micah a quick kiss on the cheek as thanks. But when Isaac entered the bedroom that night, far more wasted than usual, Ellie knew there was something wrong. Unfortunately, she wasn't in her own senses to take care of the situation appropriately. Instead, she continued to lay naked under the covers, inviting a reddening Isaac with a warm smile.

She would've expected him to leap in next to her and duck his head under the covers before she could. What she didn't expect him to do was come around to her side of the bed, spill some martini onto his covers, and grab her chin in his oversized hand. She didn't remember it being particularly painful - him holding her possessively, that was - but she remembered feeling shocked. And, if her face betrayed her, scared. With Micah, she'd never experienced anything but the gentlest of his touches. Though Isaac was, in fact, rougher than her best friend, she'd never seen him man handle anything before, much less her.

He was drunk. That explained why her loving boyfriend decided the only way to discipline her was to hit her across the face with a curled fist, with enough force to make her bang her head against the headboard.

He was drunk and angry. That explained why before and after he hit her, her charming admirer felt the need to call her a fat, unlovable whore with nothing better to do than to sell herself out to other handsome men.

He was drunk and angry and tired. That explained why once her extroverted friend was done shouting at her, his fingers threaded into the roots of her hair, he passed out across her naked body, leaving her to move him as she cried.

That was what Ellie told herself: he was drunk and angry and tired. That's what she told herself and him. And for everyone that dared to ask her what happened when they saw her reddened, then purpling, then blackened cheek, she said she'd mistakenly fallen off the bed that night, landing right on her cheek. And, as far as she knew, they all bought the lie he'd made her weave. And from then, it was that very lie that embodied her and Isaac's relationship.

It was nothing more than a mistake.

• • •

"And there you are - your drink and pesto linguini fresh out of my freezer," he said, setting a flute of champagne and a plate of pasta before her. Isaac was in a ridiculously good mood - he'd just gotten a raise in his salary. He had intended to celebrate the night with Ellie, but she beat him to the punchline far earlier. She was at his apartment before he could even lift his phone to text her. When he'd started preparing dinner for the both of them, she hadn't the heart to tell him that Friday's were for her and Micah. But when she'd left her own apartment, she couldn't bear Micah's crestfallen face as she tucked her scarf into her jacket.

Isaac was taking his seat when she said, "I told you I couldn't stay for long."

"Not even long enough for dinner? Nonsense!"

He was started digging into his food voraciously, sipping at his drink monstrously. If Ellie hadn't known him any better, she might have mistaken him for an animal. But she did know better; Isaac was only half an animal. He was still working towards a complete transformation. Three years of losing his temper and two years of hitting her didn't work a miracle like a full moon would.

"Actually, I can't stay long enough for even dinner. Micah's waiting for me."

He rolled his eyes. "Of course he is."

Ellie ran a shaking hand over her face, smearing her eyeliner and smudging her lipstick. It was one thing to accidentally mention something to Isaac, but it was a different thing to deliberately tell him, knowing the consequences. She'd spent the night before contemplating. For the first time since her and Isaac had started dating, she'd had to attend his New Year party on her own. From the looks of it, Micah and Isla were becoming awfully close since she took him to meet her family, which was expected considering how long they'd been dating. Although she was happy for them, Ellie had an inkling of fear that a proposal would be happening soon.

While she'd felt insecure without Micah by her side, the more she thought about it, the better she felt about his absence. Without him, Isaac had no reason to physically, or verbally, hurt her for her actions. That was, of course, if she kept the kiss she'd shared with Micah two weeks prior a secret. At first, she was comfortable with keeping her lips sealed; the idea of having one less black eye or swollen cheek excited her. Then she started to think again - paranoia began to set in. What if Isaac found out through Micah? What if he found out through another drunken spin the bottle? What if finding out by any means other than Ellie herself angered him more than usual? The more she got thinking, the more she realized the best way to deal with her temperamental boyfriend was honestly and fearfully.

"So why are you still here, Ellie? You've congratulated me already. I believe you have somewhere else to be now, no?"

"Yes, I do, but I actually have something else I'd like to to tell you."

"What's that?"

Ellie slowly went around to his side of the table, taking a nervous seat next to him. He refused to put down his cutlery - his knife especially - until she took them forcefully, setting them far, far away. She offered him a weathered smile when she took his hands in his, in the hopes that her sadness wouldn't show. Apparently it didn't because Isaac's face brightened like the star atop his Christmas tree. He held her hands tightly, the tattoos over his knuckles catching her eye - a symbol for each of her favorite movies. She stared at the rose under his ring finger for a second too long.

"You promise you won't get mad?"

He gave her a serious look. "I promise but, I mean, when do I ever get mad, babe?"

She didn't dare question him. "Right. So, you know how for my birthday Micah always does something big? Well, this year he toned it down a little and took me to see the new Beauty and the Beast. It was wonderful - I definitely recommend it, babe. After that, we got takeout and we were recreating the movie because why the hell not. You should've seen me, Isaac - I made a really good Gaston."

He chuckled at that, but gestured for her to continue. "Micah was just watching me for the most part, but I thought the reenactment would be better if he played the part of some of the characters. He did a marvellous job, might I add. But, we didn't think things true and we did almost every act of the movie, including the part where the beast transforms back into a prince. Long story short, we did that part of the movie and it's iconic because Belle and Adam kiss and so Micah and I kissed. You promised not to get mad though, so you're not mad. Wow, it feels good to get that off my chest."

He might've promised not to be mad, but Isaac was terrible at keeping his promises. When she looked at his face, he looked beyond livid. He shook off her grip, his hands trembling. He rubbed them together, blew on them quietly as he got to his feet. His chair dropped to the ground with a resounding thud. Just as Ellie thought he was going to walk past her and she was going to have to call out to him or, better yet, slip out of his apartment, he grabbed her by the neck of her jacket, tugging her to her feet.

"You kissed him, you said?"

"Isaac, please."

"Do you regret it? Tell me you regret it, Ellie."

When realization dawned in his eyes when she said nothing, he threw her aside like she was a rag doll. His footsteps thundered behind her as he closed the distance between them. "Get out, Ellie."

"Isaac, please listen to me." She didn't notice that the knife and fork were back in his hand. She wouldn't have said anything if she had. She'd spoken in the hopes of calming him down, not with the intention of triggering him. He lashed out just as she tried to shield her body, cutting a crimson ribbon from her wrist down to her elbow with his knife. She didn't even flinch in pain - the only thing coursing through her veins was fear.

"GET OUT!"

She didn't have to be told twice.

● ● ●

"Goddamn are you late. I'm starving, Ellie!" Micah exclaimed from his position on the kitchen counter as she shoved into their apartment. She tried to disguise the pinch in her face when she accidentally used her bad arm to push in. He gave no thought to her windblown hair, and he didn't pay any attention to her swollen eyes. When she slipped inside wordlessly, his gaze stopped at her hidden arm.

"Whatcha got there?"

"What's for dinner?" she countered.

"Why are you hiding your hand? You've got a present for me?"

"Why are you curious? Do you have a present for me?" she countered once again.

"Show me your hand, Ellie. You're acting strange."

"The same goes for you. Show me your hand."

"Is that a ketchup stain on your pants? Oh wait, it's blood."

"Is that shit on your head? Oh wait, it's hair."

Micah lept off the counter without batting an eyelash and approached her, plucking the keys out of her hand. When Ellie tried to pull away, he only tightened his grip. The more she tried to fight him, the more the sleeve of her jacket seemed to inch up. Micah seemed to bristle with anger because a vein in his neck bulged - she was waiting for the smoke to come out of his ears, but it never did. He turned away sharply, tucking the keys into his back pocket as he pushed her out of the apartment.

"Wait for me at the car," he instructed.

"Micah, I don't need the hospital; it's just a small cut. The bleeding'll stop soon."

He shrugged on his coat. "It's not the hospital I'm taking you to."

"Then where?"

"Just a boyfriend's house."

"Micah."

When he spoke, his voice was nearly as sharp as the kitchen knife Isaac had used on her. "I want you to see me when I hurt him the same way he's hurt you."

• • •

a/n: hello! so i'm here with a friday update for the first time in forever. admittedly, it's a little late in the day but here's the thing: i got a little too caught up with this show called Skam. it isn't even english guys. i'm watching a fucking norwegian show and i can't stop - it's just so addicting i can't handle it. i've got so much homework i should be doing and i've essentially neglected all of it and i'm slowly realizing how much i regret everything haha. oh well! i hope you guys liked this chapter because i mean - isaac about to get his balls busted i think. thank you all so much for reading! paper hearts hit #752 in short story the other day and i nearly died. that's INSANE! thank you guys so so much for that <3

12 | together

PAPER HEARTS | 12

warning: contains some mature content

Hospitals made him sick, but it wasn't a sickness caused by any illness passing through the air. When he pushed through the revolving doors, he was immediately hit with a wave of nausea. Micah found himself pausing at the entrance to seize a breath, but he also found that with every subsequent breath, he felt fainter. There was something about catching a whiff of impending death that made his head spin.

His father had been lying on his deathbed for months now, his lung cancer finally taking a toll on him. Micah's mother had come to terms with it - she was well enough that she could now visit the hospital every day without shedding a tear. Really, she was so well that she was already preparing herself to court another man - not that Micah cared or paid attention in the slightest. His father had also passed down the family business to Mitchell, the only one in their line who was willing to run a multi-million dollar company. While Micah had taken a liking to the engineering side of things, Mitchell had always been a businessman in the making - street smart, sly, and money hungry.

Mitchell liked to get the money, and Micah loved to spend it.

Though everyone in his family had seemed to move on forget about his father, Micah found himself driving in every other week to check up on him. If he was lucky, he only cried as his father slept. Under any other circumstance, it was his father who would wipe the tears from his cheeks. However, when even doing that little seemed to weaken him, Micah brought in backup: Ellie. Since she was even more prone to crying than he was, Micah had a feeling he could fake strength for her sake - after all, he would've felt terrible to drag her all the way to the hospital just to make her cry.

And, as it turned out, his father enjoyed Ellie's company more than his own. Micah and his father thought along the same lines, perhaps because Micah had always dreamed to be like him. Like Micah, his father thought Ellie had a knack for storytelling - talking in general actually. That was probably thanks to her writing background. Like Micah, his father found her to be beautiful with her dirty blonde hair and blue-green eyes making for an irresistible combination. It only helped her case that she was a naturally thicker girl too. Like Micah, Mr. Matthews found that when Ellie smiled, the room, and his own damned life, seemed to brighten up significantly. Something about her tinkling laughter and pearly whites were enough to make him believe that, just for a second, it wasn't life support keeping him alive.

On a day the same as any other, Micah wasn't necessarily shocked when his father beckoned for him to come closer after sending Ellie out to check with his nurse when he was due for his meds. However, much to Micah's surprise, his father snagged him by the ear and yanked him forward.

"You're going to marry this girl, right?" his father asked, hopeful.

Micah laughed; he'd never heard anything so ridiculous before. "She's nothing more than a friend!"

His father shrugged. "I'm just saying, buddy. She doesn't seem like the kind to run when things get difficult."

Micah cast a glance over his desk to catch sight of Ellie who, unsurprisingly enough, was making small talk with the petite lady at the front desk. "She's one of the bravest, strongest girls I've ever known. That's for sure."

• • •

It hadn't been difficult for Ellie to get Isaac checked into the hospital; even she had been willing to believe her own lie. With how swollen and purple his face had become, she had hardly been able to recognize him - and that was after she ignored all the blood. When a nurse had rushed up to them asking what had happened, Ellie had shrugged. She didn't know who he was; she had simply been in the park with her boyfriend, minding her own business, when she'd seen Isaac getting beat up on the football field. While her boyfriend had managed to chase away those hitting Isaac, she'd tended to his wounds and brought him to the hospital out of concern.

At least, that was what the nurse had believed.

Isaac had gazed at her as he was led away, but Ellie was quick to turn on her heels and stride out of the hospital. She had still be cradling her cut arm but, fortunately, the bleeding had stopped for the most part. As Micah had thrown Isaac about his apartment, she'd been busy tending to her own wounds. She'd given up trying to convince him to stop. She was without a care when Micah had Isaac up against a wall, the same knife her boyfriend had used to attack her pressed against his own jugular. Threats were shared and apologies were given, but both were half-assed. When Ellie got into her car, she was furious. She'd never asked for an abusive boyfriend, nor had she asked for her best friend to beat up said boyfriend. The last thing she needed was to tend to Micah's bloodied knuckles and Isaac's bloodied face.

Boys were boys and bloodying each other up was what they did best. And, as if it that wasn't enough, they had to bloody her up as well. She reeked of copper and not even the storm outside could wash away the smell.

Micah had turned all the lights in the apartment off. After he came to the conclusion that he was done with Isaac, he'd hopped into his car and had returned to their apartment without another word, leaving Ellie to tend to her nearly-dead boyfriend. She had no idea how Micah had come to know Isaac was hitting her nor was she in the right state of mind to dwell on the thought. Believing he was asleep, she was quiet as she snuck into her room to change into a dry pair of clothes. She startled when she heard her bedroom door shut with a faint click.

"He'll live?"

She didn't stop searching for a comfortable pair of pants. "Luckily, yes."

"Why is it lucky?" he snapped. "I should've killed him for what he did to you."

"No, you shouldn't have. You shouldn't have done what you did to begin with. Taking him to a hospital was one thing, but bailing you out of jail would've been another. "

"How can you lecture me after everything he's done?"

The storm had worn on into the night - a cold, starless night. But even with no lamplight or moonlight, when she turned to face him, Ellie could make out the pure, lethal rage written all over Micah's face. It didn't take a genius to imagine the knitted brows and the thin lips; the shaking fists and dark eyes. She winced when the full force of the ice in his voice hit her - the pent up anger, the unrequited hatred. She stumbled a step back just as lightning cracked, shadowing her partially naked frame, his wet head of hair.

Their hearts beat in sync to the harsh pitter-patter of the rain. They felt the thunder rumble in their chests. It was a tsunami of emotions washing over them, drowning them. An earthquake threatened to open up at their feet - swallow them. Ellie clung to the bed for support. Micah closed the distance between them, waiting for her answer.

She wondered how she hadn't totally realized just how tall he was compared to her. "Because, for whatever reason, I still love him, Micah. Because I know that somewhere, deep down, there's still the man I fell in love with."

She pushed past him, disregarding the twinge of guilt she felt when she heard him slam into her bedside. Ellie had to push down her own anger. It was his shirt she was wearing - his favorite shirt that she only wore when she was truly upset. She had to push down her shame because underneath the shirt was nothing. Her bra and underwear were soaked, and she hadn't gotten the chance to put on a fresh pair before Micah barged into her room. She bit back the tears, failing to ignore the way her thighs chafed uncomfortably.

"You can't really believe that, Ellie; tell me you don't believe that. Why would you even think of going back to that guy when there are so many other people out there who will love you and treat you far better than he will?"

A shiver scuttled down her spine. "Like who? Give me one name, and I will never go back Isaac."

He made a face. "How much more obvious do I have to make it? It's me, Ellie! I'm fucking in love with you, and you don't even realize it!"

She was at the door. Her hand was on the knob. A slight turn and a forceful push later, she could lock Micah in the room. But when the knob locked in place, a hand shot out, slamming the door back shut. Ellie felt Micah's hot breath against the nape of her neck, her collarbone. Ellie's breath shallowed, her head lolling forward.

"What do I have to do to make you love me back?" It wasn't a question; it was a plea of sorts.

Her breath caught in her throat. "Stop," she whispered. "You have a girl-friend, remember?"

Micah was relieved that she didn't say that she had a boyfriend. His hands ran up her arms, and his lower lip dragged up her neck. "She's only my girlfriend when I'm not thinking about you, and that's hardly ever."

She closed her eyes, bit down on her tongue until she was sure it would bleed. She wasn't going to hiss when his warm hand connected with the cool, shivering skin that was her bare stomach. She wasn't going to moan when his thumb grazed the underside of her breast, or flicked her nipple roughly. She wasn't going to cry out when he rolled one of those peaks between his fingers - she wasn't going to let him know that they had peaked just for him. Micah's breath hitched as she arched into him, her body pressing against his for support.

"This isn't right," she cried out, reaching for the doorknob once again. His arm was still braced against the door, though.

"I don't believe that. But if you do, Ellie, tell me to stop. Tell me where you draw the line. If you can do that, I'll leave. But if you can't ..." Micah pulled back from her so that she was staring into those deep, dark, hungry eyes of his. "If you can't tell me to stop, you're mine."

In response, Ellie slid her hands underneath his sweatshirt. Warming her icy hands was the thin sheen of sweat that had developed on his chest.

Micah stilled as her hands roamed, pausing at his stomach, at his heart, at his bicep. He shrugged his shirt off as she took a step closer, pressing a wet kiss to the curve of his shoulder.

"Isla can never find out about this."

"She won't have to." The finality of his statement made her pause her venture upwards, but before Ellie could think more into his words, Micah captured her lips with his. It started slow, with the gentle sear of passion burning through, but when their chests collided, it was as if everything else in the world fell away. Encased in their very own world, with no one existing other than them, Micah and Ellie lost themselves in each other - Micah in her touch, and Ellie in his lips.

Using the doorframe as a support, Micah hoisted her into his arms, hands settling under her thighs and encouraging her to lock her ankles around his waist. "Bed," she murmured against his lips. "Get to my bed."

She almost came undone when his tongue flicked against her earlobe. "Are you wet just for me?" A finger slid against her, teased her, tested her. "I want you to be wet for me every day. Just the thought of me should have you feeling parched, and when you can't take it anymore, I want you to think of my mouth right where you want it - doing exactly as my finger does right now."

A finger eased in, a second, a third. And this time, Ellie cried out. She bucked against him and she relished the way he groaned in her ear when she brushed against him - him. Her hand sought that kind of penance for her pleasure and when she gripped him through his pants, Micah bit down on the tender skin of her jaw. It was a rhythm between the two - with every pulse between her legs, he was digging his fingers deeper and deeper until he was sure she would crack. The more he delved past her lips, the more she pushed back against him, writhing for release. The tighter she gripped him, the darker the hickey he expected to leave.

Micah was gentle as he laid her across her bedspread, splaying her out as if she was his personal feast. She was gentle when she tangled her fingers in his hair, guiding him around her body, down her body. Ellie arched into him when he palmed her breasts, using his mouth to capture a nipple in his mouth. Ellie cried out when his head dipped past her navel, kissing the inside of her thigh before the apex of her legs. Whatever magic Micah worked on her mouth he also worked on the quivering spot between her legs.

But, for the first time, Micah wasn't the only one pleasuring. As he brought her down from her high, she twisted, turning him onto his back.

He squeezed his eyes tight, his hands fisted into the sheets until she was done taking every inch, every ounce, of him into her mouth.

He remained on his back as he took her hands in his and guided her onto his lap, one leg settled on each side of his torso. He sat up, cupping the back of her neck when he pulled her in for a kiss. It was like a sailor salvaging his last breath of air before he went under for the last time. It was desperate; it was forceful; it was desirous, and greedy, and ravenous. Micah growled every time she caressed his lips with hers, every time she writhed against him, waiting. Ellie moaned loudly, gasped, when he sucked her tongue into his mouth.

"Do you want me to stop, Ellie?"

When she didn't respond, he guided himself to her entrance and with one quick thrust, entered her. Ellie didn't scream, nor did she try to kiss him. She met his eyes with every subsequent thrust; she matched his smile with her own, her nails digging into his back to maintain balance.

"Together?" she asked.

They didn't come back from their high. They didn't recover from the head-spinning or the sweating or the soreness. Not five minutes or ten minutes or an hour later.

Not for the rest of the night.

• • •

a/n: phew! that was a difficult chapter to write for sure. that being said, i hope you guys enjoyed! the last 2-3 chapters have been fairly longer than usual but i promise they'll go back to their normal length soon enough. i'm officially on spring break so i'm hoping to get some writing done. in my mind, i see myself finishing paper hearts and getting a start on ghost or sweet talks - either of the two haha. we'll have to see if i stick to that plan. thank you all so so so much for getting paper hearts to rank in Short Story!! that's absolutely huge and i'm so honored for all of you reading and supporting this story! and, if you hadn't seen it, i posted the sequel to paper hearts! yup, that's right - a sequel. i've made a couple of edits and i've decided to make this a 3-part series. the next book - stolen hearts - will be featuring micah's brother, mitchell, and i'm super super excited for it. stolen hearts will be updated with a character trailer + cast later today. so, if you're interested, go check out stolen hearts and lemme know what you think! and again, as always guys, thank you so much for reading <3

13 | athenian

PAPER HEARTS | 13

"How about a wedding in California? We could do one of those beach ones. Good weather is a guarantee.

She shook her head. Too local.

"Fine, then what about a wedding on a cruise? We could go to the bahamas or something. It would be an all-you-can-eat buffet and enough water slides to last you a lifetime."

She made a face. Too many strangers, and she'd likely eat her way to three sizes above her wedding dress.

"Athens - I promise you Percy Jackson will be there."

She giggled, nudging Isaac's shoulder. "Why do I need Percy when I have you?"

"You're a flirt, I see," he responded, nudging her back.

They'd met for the first time on Halloween day a year ago. It was an October night blessed with a sky full of constellations for the children to marvel over and a full moon, allowing for the werewolves to transform. It was a night laced with frost; the cold seeping in through my pores and chilling me to the bone. It was a night embroidered by a breeze; the gust sending strong shivers rumbling through my spine. As premature as Ellie liked to think Isaac was for thinking about a marriage, she was glad she'd found someone who wanted just as grand of a wedding as her.

They were lying in his backyard, under a starless sky. Ellie lifted a trembling finger into the air, tracing the patterns the stars created while Isaac memorized her face for the millionth time that night. He ran a hand down the sharp lines of her cheeks, over the smooth skin that was her pink lips and through her hair, which was embroidered with stray leaves and dirt. Even though he'd laid out a blanket, Ellie had somehow rolled off.

Learning how to live among nature was what she called it. Isaac didn't want to burst her bubble by saying she was barely ten feet away from his back door - in other words, a refrigerator filled with food, a room with an air mattress and television and most important of all, a toilet. He briefly recalled the last time I took her camping. Ellie had refused to pee in the bushes so she'd held it in for a day in a half before she'd finally peed in her shorts. She'd run out of clean shorts to wear two days into the seven day trip and when it came to the other business, she gave him no choice but to drive her to the nearest gas station.

It was as she rolled onto her side that she realized they were, potentially, stupidly, madly, hilariously in love with each other. Isaac could never seem to get enough of her voice, calling her in the middle of the night and then in the middle of her classes. He always found a way to sneak into her dormitory and steal a kiss from her in between classes - something about her lips and her breasts had him coming back for more. According to his friends, he talked about her enough for them to start avoiding his company. He was obsessed, and she loved the attention wholly.

He wasn't a half bad boyfriend, or specimen, himself. He always greeted her in his dorm with a warm cup of hot chocolate and a single pink marshmallow. Ellie liked to joke that if it weren't for his barista-like skills and his dazzling smile, she wouldn't be with him - Isaac complained that the comment made him awfully insecure. She didn't believe him. For someone who could dance on a restaurant table without being drunk, she doubted a teasing comment would make him question the entirety of his existence.

"There must be more than this provincial life," she sighed.

"There is. Just watch. I'm going to make you my wife."

Ellie gagged. "Can you imagine! Me? The wife of your boorish, brainless... Madame Bowman? Absolutely not."

"Oh, so are you going to have that Athenian wedding with someone else?"

"You make a solid case for yourself, Isaac Bowman."

His lip caught between his teeth, a hand drifted over his waist and tugged her onto his chest. Ellie fell atop of him with a gasp, praying that the sudden impact of her weight wouldn't snap him in half.

Isaac didn't flinch.

"Of course I do, darling. I'll be fighting for that wedding until my dying breath," he promised.

Although she hadn't believe him, as it turned out, he hadn't necessarily been lying.

• • •

For the first time in her life, she was finally finished writing a story of hers. Matter of fact, she was finished proof-reading the manuscript and Ellie was ready to send it back to her publishers. Neither her family nor Micah knew about her accomplishment, or her potentially nearing success. She was ready to leave the life of a registered nurse and get back to writing full-time - the only other time she'd ever been able to do so was in high school when it seemed like she didn't have a life outside of her fantasies, both in her head and on paper.

Calla Ardelene, the girl Ellie could only dream of being, was finally going to be a reality if everything went according to her plan. It was less of the character and more of her story that Ellie was invested in. As it turned out, as her relationships with Micah and Isaac progressed, so did Calla's relationship with the day and the dark. Her head told her to go with the one she could see - the one she'd learned to love. Her head told her that predictability was good; familiarity was even better, and she'd never been more familiar with anyone other than the daily rising sun.

No matter how warm it was, no matter how intense it was, no matter how painful it was to be near it, Calla's mind forced her forward. It wanted her to throw herself into the fire and in the midst of it all, it hoped she would return unburned.

But there was also her heart attempting to do some thinking of its own. It wanted everything she couldn't have. It wanted anything it knew could cause more harm than good. It knew that whatever it fell for, no matter how kind or loving it was, Calla would never go after it because, as far as she knew, her heart could never overpower her head. The same went for Ellie. Her heart yearned for one thing, but her head told her something else.

Her heart deserved kindness; her head thought it was beastliness she asked for.

When a knock echoed through the apartment, she expected to see a groomed Micah waiting on the other side of the door. She stumbled back when she came face-to-face with a still bruised, still battered Isaac. The swelling had gone down significantly but she had a feeling his black eye would take far longer than a week to fade away. Now that the blood had been cleaned away, Ellie could make out the collateral damage - the split eye and the cut on his cheek, the bruise on his collarbone and the hunch in his stance.

"Hi," he said weakly.

Ellie backed up and was about to slam the door shut when his foot shot out. She heard a crack, but neither flinched. "I won't be long, Ellie. Give me five minutes. May I come in?"

"No. Whatever you have to say can be said out here, and you can say it all in two minutes."

She considered telling him about her and Micah having sex. The thought made her smile inwardly - he couldn't move without limping, or wheezing. What was he going to do? Was he going to try to lunge for her if she told him about how they'd had sex multiple times during his stay at the hospital? Was he going to try to hit her if she told him that Micah could pleasure her better than he ever had? Ellie would've liked to see him try.

"I was a monster - I realize that now. Whatever I did was wrong and I know that no matter how hard I try, I won't be able to get you to forgive me. I wouldn't want you to forgive me when I can't even forgive myself."

Lies.

"But you remember the first night we talked about getting married? When we were still in college? I never stopped thinking about that - I never once stopped thinking about marrying you. The night you came to my place after I got the raise... I had another reason for wanting you to stay for dinner. It wasn't a romantic setting or anything, but if our wedding was going to be so grand, I didn't think you'd care if the proposal wasn't as nice."

Isaac fished out out a black velveteen box from his jacket pocket and held it out to her. He didn't do anything; he didn't say anything. One hand behind his neck and the other outstretched, he waited until she took the box from him with shaky fingers. Ellie couldn't look him in the eye.

"You don't have to say anything to me right now. Think about it - take as much time as you need. I'd like for you to make me the happiest man in the world, but if you decide it's best we part ways, I'll - I'll understand, Ellie."

The box was heavy. She could imagine the diamond waiting to sit on her ring finger.

"Please marry me, Ellie. Let our Athenian wedding become a reality."

She slammed the door shut.

Ellie waited until she heard retreating footsteps before she sank to the floor. The box remained unopened in her palms; the box would remain unopened, or so she thought.

Her head was telling her otherwise.

• • •

a/n: this is totally unedited so i'm super super sorry for any grammatical errors. on a totally different note though, paper hearts is finally completed! wow did this take a long time. a little dedication this week and i finally managed to finish it and i'm kinda happy with the way it turned out. i hope you guys think so too. that being said, what did you guys think about this chapter? do drop a comment below and let me know! thank you so so much to everyone reading this story. your guys's constant support has been beyond amazing and i can't thank you guys enough for that. now, i'm off to go start riverdale (or continue to catch up on GoT), hehe.

14 | worthy

[dedicated to as a sincere thank you for reading this story. a new reader always warms my heart so thank you so much for taking the time to give this story a chance <3]

PAPER HEARTS | 14

Ellie's first interaction with Isla was two months into her relationship with Micah. It was the first time he'd brought her back to their apartment for dinner, but it wasn't the first time Ellie had seen her. Isla didn't remember very well, but Ellie had met her at the same Christmas party where Micah had met her, and Isla had looked radiant as ever. Aside from thinking about how much she wanted to look like her, Ellie had also thought about what a great pair her and Micah would've made.

Fire and ice, she thought. He was one to get lost in the passion of a relationship and, from the way Isla handled herself, she seemed like the type to soothe in a necessary practicality. They contrasted each other perfectly - an idealist to a realist; a fierce desire turned growing love to an admiration turned undeniable attraction.

It was by no means an awkward dinner. While Ellie hadn't felt comfortable talking to begin with, Micah, as always, was the necessary extrovert in her life. He'd eased her into conversation, and Isla had carried it from there on out, telling tales of her childish rebellions while requesting stories about Ellie's academic tribulations. They were complete opposites, as it turned out. Isla had been an idiosyncratic problem child while Ellie had been the golden girl - nonetheless, both girls had grown up to represent some semblance of the same person.

It was half hour into dinner when Micah had to leave abruptly on some office work - something along the lines of a launch failure.

While Micah had offered to drop her home, Isla had politely declined, saying she wanted to spend a little more time with Ellie and, perhaps, get to know her. It took all of Ellie's self control to keep from beaming too much. Growing up, she hadn't been one to make or have many friends. Back in the day, she'd matched Isla's alleged quirkiness, but while hers was welcomed, most thought Ellie's eccentricities were odd. No matter how much she tried to change her behaviors to appeal to others, it seemed like the other kids were always one step ahead of her, changing what they did and what they liked before she could.

Naturally, she'd grown into a shell, and she'd never learned to break out of it. The fear of being rejected stayed with her, and that kept Ellie from going out and trying to meet new people, make new friends. She waited for them to come to her, and she'd come to realize that even if they didn't come, she was going to be alright. She'd been alright without many, if any, friends since her elementary years, and she figured she'd continue to be fine for as long as she needed. But, when someone did seem like they could be an unexpected friend, she never stopped her heart from swelling.

"So," Isla started. "I don't want you to think this will be the basis of our friendship - if you choose to be friends with me, that is. I don't want to force you or anything. But I have to ask - are you and Micah just friends or do you guys have a friends with benefits thing going?"

Ellie's eyebrows rose just as her poorly chewed tomato when down the wrong pipe. Isla panicked, scrambling for water and potentially the Heimlich maneuver as Ellie simultaneously laughed and choked. "Friends, Isla," she spluttered. "We're just friends."

She laughed, falling back in her seat. "Well, now that that's cleared up..."

"Do you wanna watch a movie?" Ellie asked.

"I hope your definition of movie is equivalent to a chick flick."

Ellie smiled. "I think we're gonna get along very well."

• • •

Sometimes Isla stopped by for just lunch whenever she needed someone to keep her company on a slow day. But, if there was ever a day where Isla wasn't feeling it, it was likely Ellie was faring even worse. On those days, even small talk was pushing it. While the two liked to think it was a magical occasion full of bonding, in reality, they usually ate their lunches in silence, asked a few questions to catch up on the day's gossip, and then parted ways.

But when both Ellie and Isla were having good days, they always had fun times. Whether it was going out for lunch or going to the mall for a cheap shopping spree, the afternoons were always full of horrible inside jokes, usually at Micah's expense, and questionable tastes in fashion or food. Micah liked to call them stupid, but, in each other's defense, it was risque.

Ellie always looked forward to those kind of afternoons - they were almost enough to make up for the years she'd missed out on knowing what it would be like to hang out with actual friends.

What Ellie and Isla craved throughout the week varied; some days it was Chinese express, and others it was classic Italian. Most Friday's however, they were rushing the small Middle Eastern restaurant in its secluded corner of downtown. It was a local restaurant run by family of four, and while prices were usually on the higher end, everything was freshly made, hand made, and well worth it. Since the two were regular visitors, the family was kind enough to give them a package of falafels to go, alongside their already hefty order of tabouleh, shawarma and shish tawook.

That afternoon, Isla wasn't acting awkward but shopping and eating aside, Ellie could tell something was bothering her. "Got something on your mind?"

She shrugged. "Just the usual. You and Micah, me and Micah." She paused. "You and Isaac."

They were seated at a booth towards the very back of the restaurant, away from the kitchen, away from the noise. While Ellie was practically inhaling her food, Isla was pushing hers around her plate. Usually, it was the other way around. "How'd you know about Isaac?"

"I didn't know anything; I just had a hunch. That last conversation - you put up a lot of red flags. I had my doubts so I told Micah to keep an eye out for your behavior when you'd return from Isaac's place. Turns out he didn't have to."

The duo laughed at the last part, but when their smiles died down, so do their conversation. Silence blanketed them, and though Ellie opened her mouth repeatedly as if to say something, the words kept getting stuck in her throat. She wanted to ask Isla if Micah had told her about what they'd done that night. She wanted to apologize to Isla for everything they'd done, she'd done. Ellie wanted to tell Isla that maybe there was an actual reason to her having no friends - more of a reason than just her being odd. Maybe she didn't have friends because people could tell that she couldn't be trusted - that she'd have sex with their boyfriends behind their backs.

"He told me that he thinks he loves you, you know."

When Ellie said nothing, Isla continued. "He says he doesn't know for sure, but he thinks he's in love with you more than he is with me. It hurt. A lot. But I've always just wanted him to be happy, and if being in love with you is what makes him happy, there's nothing I can do about it."

"You really do love him, don't you?"

Isla nodded. "It's stupid, I know. After everything you guys have done - after this! I know I shouldn't love him. I know I should maybe even hate him for leading me on, but I can't. He's been good to me all these years. He's loved me like no one else, and he's treated me probably better than my own family. He's the realest gentleman there is out there and it's for that reason that I can't bring myself to hate him. When you love him as much as I do... Loving him is like breathing; it's as easy as breathing. But falling out of love with him - it won't be that simple."

Isla's head lifted. The steel in her stormy eyes sparkled Despite a sadness humming through her body, her eyes were still like a puddle of starlight; thick like oil, warm like the fire running under her skin, bright like a streaming ray of sunlight. In that moment, Ellie was was Isla's reflection - torn, heartbroken, confused.

"How do you still forgive him after everything he's done?"

"For the longest time, I didn't think I'd find anyone. I didn't think anyone would love me because I thought I was a horrible person. That boyfriend who kicked me out of my apartment? I never told you why he did it." With that, Isla looked down at her plate. "It was a mistake. I'd started to get paranoid that he was hooking up with other girls behind my back and I thought that if he was allowed to do it and I had to be okay with, I figured I could do the same. Well, I slept with another man and my boyfriend found out, and surprise, surprise - he wasn't sleeping with anyone else. It was just me letting my insecurities get the best of my thoughts.

"When I first started dating Micah, I thought I was lucky. I thought I was blessed to be given a second chance, and I promised myself that I'd be different. I swore I wouldn't be paranoid, even if he was sharing a place with his best friend, who was a girl. And, in reality, I didn't have to be because you guys were almost always honest about telling me what you two did together - sexually and otherwise. I thought I should break up with him. I considered it for a really long time, but Micah coming into my life was my second chance. I thought he also deserved one.

"I'd done the same thing with another man as you two have. I didn't think I was worthy of another relationship; I thought I deserved to have a boyfriend who loved another girl more than he loved me."

Ellie made a face, reaching across the table to take Isla's chilled hands. There were tears in both their eyes when Ellie spoke. "You are worthy of a better relationship. You are deserving of someone who loves you. We all are."

Isla managed a smile, but it hardly met her eyes. "I know that now, but - the funny thing is, I don't want anything better anymore. I just want him." The tears were falling freely now. "God! This is the saddest fucking relationship ever. I must sound ridiculous for wanting it."

"No, you're not stupid for wanting it." Ellie paused, her eyes squeezed shut. "I'm stupid for trying to take it away from you."

• • •

a/n: if you find any grammatical errors, i apologize for that! i did read this once before officially posting but i could've missed something - this chapter had missing words everywhere haha. anyway, i hope you guys enjoy this part! there are only 2 more after this so i'm super super excited for you guys to read those! i believe my next project once this is completed will be sweet talks (since i've got the story planned completely) but i likely will not start writing it until mid may. on a completely different note - guys. i finished game of thrones today and i'm a wreak - i no longer know what to do with myself. at first, i wasn't too into the show. it was just alright up until season 3 but once season 4 started... holy shit. it got so freaking good. what am i supposed to do without this show now? what was my life before game of thrones wtf. but again, thank you all so so much for reading! as always, it means the world to me <3

15 | fire

[dedicated to because they've been reading this story from the very start and i should've dedicated a part to them a long, long time ago - it's just a way of showing my appreciation for your continuous support. thank you for everything <3]

PAPER HEARTS | 15

She'd worshipped Isaac the same way she'd worshipped one too many people in her life. She adored the way his biceps curled when they went to the gym together and he sat her on his lap as they lifted weights. She adored the way he twirled her in the middle of a busy sidewalk during their summer days because he wanted to see her dress float with the dead breeze; he wanted to bring a smile to her face. She adored the way he looked at her when he took her to clubs just to have an excuse to dance with her all night long. She adored his parents, his puppy, his philanthropy, his kindness, his laugh, his devotion, him.

What they had at the start was beautiful, but beauty never came without a price.

She hated the way he tightened his grip around her waist when he noticed her gaze wandering about the gym. She hated the way he accused her of flirting when her hand brushed another man's pinkie in the middle of a bustling street. She hated the way he picked a fight every time someone approached her at the club asking for a dance. She noticed the way his parents fussed over him whenever they visited; she noticed the way his puppy Max only ever approached her. She noticed the way he only donated money when she mentioned a good cause; she noticed the way he was kindest when it was only the two of them. She noticed the way he only really laughed whenever he was drunk; she noticed the way his eyes went every which way with other girls.

Isaac was two different halves of a person. His good and his bad were separated by a defined line, and he had yet to discover a way of being both at once. When he was good, he was at his best, but when he was bad, he was a beast.

That was why she'd found it so easy to fall out of love with Isaac and fall in love with Micah.

Micah's presence itself was enough for at least her heart to understand that it deserved better. The lightness in his eyes and the brightness of his personality gave her just enough strength to bury some semblance of her love for Isaac. While she still clung to Isaac for support - out of hope - she found herself going to Micah for solace - out of habit.

She'd been going to Micah since the day they'd moved in together.

In college, Ellie was used to waking up at six in the morning, but it wasn't like sleeping was easy in her dorm room. The pillows felt like they were made of bricks. The bipolarity of the temperature was to both extremes - either she was sleeping in the nude or with a parka and seventeen pairs of socks on her feet. Ellie was sure she had seen math textbooks softer than her mattress. One of the upsides of renting an already-furnished apartment was that when she'd laid eyes on the queen-sized mattress in the "master bedroom", she'd known the room would have to be hers. The downside was that she wasn't the only one who wanted it.

As much as Micah had wanted the dated bathroom and the general space, he'd known that, at the end of the day, he would've given it up if it would've made Ellie happy. It was one thing to take a bed from a girl; it was a completely different story to deprive her of her walk-in closet.

When she'd hopped onto his back screaming, "This room is mine!" Micah had been gentle to flip her onto the bed and onto her back. Only Micah would've wrestled with her for an hour only to throw his hands up in surrender right before dinner. When it came to Ellie, only Micah was willing to give her what she wanted, when she wanted it, and how she wanted it.

Even if he hated it.

• • •

When Micah returned from work on an unsuspecting Friday night, with two boxes of pizza and a bouquet of flowers for Ellie, he entered their apartment under the impression that Ellie would be sitting at their kitchen table working on the finishing touches for her manuscript. His brows knitted together when he found her crying on the couch. She flinched away from his touch when he kneeled before her, pizza set aside but flowers still in hand. Micah's own eyes teared up when he took in her reddened cheeks and swollen eyes.

"Talk to me," he murmured, running a hand up and down her bare leg. "What's wrong?"

"We can't be friends anymore."

The wildfire. It was burning - growing and spreading and devouring. For weeks, their skin had been alight, together and separate, and the heat of the flame had just begun to melt through flesh. Ellie and Micah were stuck in what they'd created, surrounded by nothing but the mess they'd managed to make. And there it was - the first ash amongst the embers. They were finally facing the ruination they should've faced long, long ago. First their skin, then their bones, then their hearts. Paper or steel, it didn't matter. When the fire died away, there'd be nothing left of the hearts to salvage.

Ellie was going to make sure of it.

"You're scaring me." Both of Micah's hands were on her legs now and their faces were leveled. His lower lip quivered when he said, "You can't just say something like that and expect me to leave it alone."

Just as much as they were fire - the chemical combination of oxygen and everything else meant to destroy - they were also water - the colorless, tasteless, odorless liquid meant to drown. Day by day, minute by minute, and second by second, Ellie and Micah drifted further away from shore until they were counting on tired limbs and fleeting fish to keep their heads above water. Truth and reality were sickening, but the weight of both on their shoulders seemed to dip them deeper into a blackening current. It wasn't a game anymore - it was becoming a battle to see how could survive the sea the longest, but Ellie had a dirty way of fighting. The longer she cried, the slower Micah kicked. The quicker he began to give in. The less he had a reason to fight.

He took a big gulp of water, and he swallowed.

"You're not making any sense, Ellie. Why can't we be friends anymore? What happened?"

"We fell in love! That's what happened, Micah! Love ruined this friend-ship."

The calm Micah was gone. The Micah Ellie had gotten to know and love was gone, and in his place was a shell of a man. A man broken by the loss of his father, his own indecision when it came to the two people he loved the most, and, finally, his best friend's betrayal. It was a nail in the coffin for him. Ellie could see it in his eyes - he wasn't sure what he was fighting for anymore. Micah could only fight for a friendship when some form of it remained between him and Ellie, but with her so convinced that it was dead, there was no resurrecting it from his end.

"Love doesn't ruin friendships, Ellie." His voice was deadly calm. "People ruin friendships. Don't do this."

"Look at where that's gotten us. It's turned us into horrible people! We kiss, and we convince ourselves it's just as friends. Fine, maybe friends do that. We have sex, and we're convincing ourselves that it's okay. Friends don't do that Micah - especially not when they're romantically involved with someone else."

What game was she playing at? Micah's eyes searched her face as if they held all the answers he needed but Ellie looked at everything but him. The way she snagged her lower lip between her teeth made it seem like she was scrambling for an argument against him. Micah wasn't angry with Ellie for trying to stop whatever was going on between them, but he was weary - he'd come to realize that she only acted oddly when Isaac or Isla were thrown into the mix.

He should've known from the first day Isaac had hit her. No matter how hungover, Ellie and Micah always dealt with their headaches together, even if each other's company made the piercing pain even worse. That morning, she hadn't left her room. When Micah had forced his way in, she had neither lifted her left face from her pillow nor had she pulled the covers down. For dinner, when she was finally on her feet, Micah had found a broken bottle of foundation on the floor when he feigned a bathroom break.

The foundation was still wet, and she hadn't gone in for her rotation that day.

"Are you saying this because of Isla? You're scared she's going to find out? Ellie, I can and I will break up with her if that's the problem."

"You've been saying that for the last two weeks yet you still string her along! You can't break up with her. You won't break up with her, and you know why that is? It's because you're in love with her!"

"I'm in love with you!"

If he'd said that with any more fierceness , any more despair, she would've believed him. Ellie, though, knew a thing or two about the heart and she knew that when it was doing the thinking instead of the head, it had a way of making people do funny things; say funny things; think funny things.

She shook her head, and when she spoke, her words came out carefully - calculated. "You're in love with Isla, Micah. You're in love with her and you're in love with the idea of me. Whatever you feel for me is not love; it's infatuation."

"You're wrong." He yanked her to her feet and without waiting, dragged her behind him. Ellie tripped over her feet and collided into his back multiple times as he led her into his bedroom but Micah didn't let up. He said nothing and he silenced all her protests as he tore through his dresser, throwing clothes aside and then the entire drawer. Under any other circumstance, Ellie would've laughed if his boxers had hit her square in the face as they had.

A hand shot to her mouth when he thrust a square box towards her.

It looked exactly like the velveteen box Isaac had given her the week before.

Micah was wild; his eyes held enough crazy to make her legs lock. He got down on a knee, fumbling to open the box and reveal a diamond engagement ring. Ellie didn't realize just how much he was hurting until a tear dripped down his cheek as he scooted towards her. "I bought this for Isla, but I couldn't give it to her, Ellie. We make each other happy. I can't tell you I'm happier any other time than when I'm with you. I'm in love with you, Ellie. I can't see myself with anyone but you, and I didn't realize that until now. I'm sorry it took so long."

"Micah - I wish you hadn't."

"Why? Does this scare you? I'm all in, Ellie. I swear to you."

"Are you kidding me? This isn't love, Micah! You're obsessed! Do you understand why you're giving me this? You're scared of me leaving you so you're doing whatever you have to to convince me to stay. That's desperation."

Micah followed her out to her room where she already had a pull-on packed up. He grabbed her wrist and spun her around when she went to reach for her suitcase.

"Don't do this," he pleaded.

"By the end of the week, either you move in with Isla, or I move out. It doesn't matter what way this goes, but I won't let this continue."

"Are you actually doing this? Are you seriously ending our friendship for my relationship? Fuck - what the fuck did Isla say to you? I'm not in love with her! It's you and me till the end, remember? Don't leave me - please, Ellie."

She tried to shoulder her way past him. Micah bolted for her door, shutting it quickly and barricading her inside with his body. She slammed her fists against his chest. He didn't move. He didn't flinch. Micah only took a step to the side when she withdrew her hand, her palm stinging and his cheek reddening. He stared at her wide-eyed, confused since she'd never hit him out of anything but humor.

Tears were freely streaming down her face. She wanted to do nothing more than to massage his cheek, touch the wound away. Kiss the pain away.

"Where's your heart? What happened to it?" His voice cracked.

"You tell me, Micah - you're the one who has it."

With that, she walked out.

• • •

a/n: hello hello! so, yeah, i sorta sunk #millie - oops. i think some of you saw it coming, haha. but, there's still another chapter so for those of you to want micah and ellie to last, there's still a chapter of hope left. but what did you guys think of this? i don't know, i really wanted to portray anger, and sadness, and confusion and i hope i could do that, haha. also! i want to thank you all so so SO much for getting paper hearts to #125 in short story earlier this week. my mind was absolutely blown and i was so thankful for every single one of you - all of you guys are the best and are blessings, i swear to god. thank you all for sticking around this long for ellie and micah's relationship, and i hope you guys do agree with whatever ending i decide for this story - i thought about what i wanted to do with them for quite a long time haha. if you have any questions as to why i've done this, feel free to drop a comment below! even if you don't have any questions, i always enjoy a comment haha. anyway, thank you all for reading <3

16 | resolution

[dedicated to and for being such fantastic readers because neither i nor this story would be where it is without your guys's love and support. thank you so so much for being so wonderful <3]

PAPER HEARTS | 16

TWO YEARS LATER

The day she'd walked out of Micah's life was the day she'd finished the slowest, longest chapter of her life. When she read it over, thought about it more, Ellie began to realize why readers preferred substance over sex. Love had to be characterized evenly by a physical connection and a mental stability, but when touch, taste, and sight becomes the foundation of a relationship, the chemical makeup of it goes awry. When the scales are tipped in favor of contact, the brain conforms to the seduction of lust. Lust doesn't lead to love; it leads to obsession.

Ellie had scrapped that chapter, crumpling it and chucking it into some unforeseen corner of her new home. Remembrance came with nostalgia - the constant revisitation of past events out of fear of forgetting them. She didn't want to remember. The key to moving on is accepting the past, and Ellie knew that if she accepted the past, she wouldn't want to move on; she knew she'd go back to him. So she created a new means of moving on - she would forget.

She would forget Micah and Isaac and Isla. She would forget every Bowman Bash and every Fuzzy Friday and every birthday celebration.

She wanted to start anew and that she did.

Without Micah by her side at every second, Ellie found that her productivity increased tenfold. She was back in nursing school during the day in the hopes of being a registered nurse. While her parents helped her to keep her single-bedroom apartment, her savings as a nurse assistant and her publications kept her from being kicked out of school. While money had been a problem when her book was first published, as the months had gone by, the income had begun to roll in steadily. She was, in some sense, making enough to keep the water and electricity running. Cable was a different story. And though Ellie had enough time in everyday to balance writing and studying, she realized that the lack of company made her feel as if there were one too many hours to each day.

She might have been getting more work done, but she wasn't enjoying any of it.

When she'd been with Micah, she'd been living, and without him, she was only existing. Things she used to find fun no longer seemed as appealing when she did them alone. In some sense, he'd ruined her in ways she hadn't realized. Ellie had become so dependent on his presence, on him, that she didn't know who she was. When they'd first parted ways, she'd feared she'd become nothing without him - the hole his absence left in her chest couldn't be filled by any family member or any new friend.

Empty - that's how it felt to leave someone who had started to become her world, as problematic as that was.

Ellie had thought the published life would be a little more glamorous than it really was. She was hoping that being a New York Times bestseller would provide her with enough to quit her assistant job and write full time, but her five seconds of fame were short lived. There were demands for a sequel, and when she announced that she would be writing one, press moved onto the next biggest author. If she wanted her spotlight back - if she wanted to be making banks - her next book would have to be a hit, just like the first one. She'd have to make it bigger and better, if she was writing for the crowd; if she was writing for herself, she'd have to trust her gut and write what she wanted to write, not what others expected her to write.

On a regular weekday, aside from driving to the community college, the furthest Ellie moved was to the bathroom and back. She kept a mini-refrigerator for frozen foods and a microwave in her bedroom itself. Weekends were a different story. With the steady silence of her home unnerving her by the end of the week, Ellie usually found herself seated in a corner booth of their local coffee shop, Coffee for Two. Given how often she visited and the haphazard state she usually visited in, Jules, the owner, always made her drink on the house. And, if she could find a few minutes to herself, she joined Ellie at her booth to listen to the author read what she'd managed to write in the hour which was, usually, nothing.

Thanksgiving felt odd. Ellie couldn't place a finger on what was putting the weight on her chest, but something wasn't right. She'd initially planned on going to her parent's place for celebrations, but they broke it to her a little too late that they'd already booked vacation tickets without her. While Ellie had wanted to throw a fit, she knew she couldn't - they were already being so patient with supporting her even though she was that one late bloomer in college. When she'd asked any of the girls in her pathophysiology class if they'd wanted to go out to have dinner at her place, all of them had declined, claiming they already had plans.

So, Ellie was spending Thanksgiving on her own at the only coffee shop to be open. It reassured her that Jules was just as friendless as she was. However, when she arrived for her regular cup of hot chocolate to sit at her regular seat to get her regular amount of writing done, Ellie had to pause because her routine had been disrupted. Jules was nowhere to be seen; instead her assistant Lia was holding out her drink. When Ellie turned to take her seat, there was someone already seated there, much to her dismay.

Her heart thunked. Stubble dashed his reddened cheeks and a pink hue had returned to his lips. She couldn't move her legs. He picked at the woolen front of his beanie, his brown hair just starting to brush the tips of his ears. She liked the look of longer hair on him. His eyes were trained on the platter of cake pops before him, as if he were counting the number of sprinkles on each one. She couldn't say she would've been surprised if he was. When their eyes met, Ellie realized just how much control Micah had over her. It was because of his smile that she put one foot in front of the other. It was because of his stupid milk mustache that she tried to return his smile. It was because of the familiar curves of his body and the way he engulfed her in a bear hug that she began to remember everything she'd tried so hard to forget.

"What brings you here on Thanksgiving day?" she asked as she took a seat across from him. She didn't make a move to remove her laptop from her bag. No matter how long the encounter lasted, she wasn't going to be getting any work done.

He took a bite out of a cake pop, the crusty frosting sticking to his teeth and the golden sparkles lining his lips. "I actually came to talk to you. I come on weekends every once in a while and I've always seen you here - I figured I'd actually try to catch you today."

"Why did you never try to catch me before?"

Micah shrugged. "Either I'd be in a rush, or you'd be writing, or you'd be talking to Jules. It never seemed like I had an opportune moment to interrupt."

Pushing the plate towards her, Micah beckoned for her to take one. Ellie shook her head and instead opted to say, "So...how have you been? It's been a while."

"Good, actually!" he replied. "Calm, I guess. After our little fall out, I really just focused on the job. I considered going back to college to get a masters in business but then I thought eh. I'm too lazy for that kind of stuff, ya know? But otherwise, I haven't been up to much. Life isn't as adventurous as it used to be, but it's a pleasant change. You, though! You're a published author! I'm so proud of you, Ellie."

She perked. "You read the book?"

He shook his head. "Unfortunately not. We have the copy at home, but I've never actually picked it up. Too many memories."

"Who's we?"

"Right, that's actually why I wanted to meet you today," he said as he reached next to him, picked up a black envelope and handed it to her. "Isla and I have been living together for a year now. After everything that happened, I moved back in with my parents because she wanted a break. Some months of couple's therapy and intense hounding later, she was willing to give me another chance and I've been making it work ever since."

Ellie's mouth went dry. As horrible as the realization felt, she knew that she'd wanted to hear that Micah and Isla had broken up. She knew she'd wanted to hear him say that he was just as hung over her as she was him. Ellie had to fight down the vomit rising in her throat when she pulled out a pristine, rose-gold colored wedding invite. She wasn't sure whether or not to laugh - she'd been pitying herself for two years while Micah had managed to move on and rebuild a messy relationship, probably all even before her book hit stores.

"When Isla asked for a break, I gave it to her but it killed me everyday that I was away. It was a different kind of thinking than you, though. Whenever I thought about you, it was because I wanted to know what it would be like to kiss you, or hold you, or be with you - as odd as that sounds. But with Isla - I just missed her. I couldn't bring myself to get over her despite knowing she could end things between us at any second. Was I really in love with you if I was over you within weeks, Ellie?"

Ellie sealed the envelope and handed it back to him crisper than when it was handed to her. "Take it back."

"You think you can come?" The hope in his voice broke her heart.

"It's not a question of whether I can come. It's a question of whether I will or won't, and I won't be coming."

"Don't do this. I feel like there's bad blood between us, and there doesn't have to be any."

"Micah-"

"I would've thought that you'd be the first to get over it, but you're not and I can't bring myself to accept that because you were the one who did this. You did this to yourself, Ellie, and maybe things wouldn't have been as bad if you'd just waited -"

Ellie raised a hand to shut him up. "If I'd just waited for what, Micah?" she challenged. "For you to continue to fall in love with me? For you to realize you weren't in love with me? If I'd let you go on thinking however you were thinking, you would've gone mad. You would've ruined your relationship with Isla and ours wouldn't have lasted and you know why? It wouldn't have lasted because you would've truly loved another girl. You would've gone back to her. And you know why this fallout was so easy for you but not for me? While you and Isla turned out to be a fucking match made in heaven, I had nobody! Isaac was dead to me, and in realizing that, I realized he'd been dead to me for years now - I had eyes for only you."

"Only for me," he echoed.

"That's right. All those years, you were my shoulder, my protector, and my friend and I couldn't stop myself. That's why I chose to stop you. I wasn't going to let you continue to think I was the one for you when you were clearly meant to be with someone else. And it was the right decision to make - look at you. You're getting married, Micah!"

"But you're not over me. You're not happy."

Ellie reached across the table, palm face up. Their fingers entwined when Micah met her halfway, and she rose from her seat to press a kiss to the back of his hand. "I've never had the chance to be on my own. When my relationship with Gavin ended, I had you to fill the void. When my relationship with Isaac ended, I still had you. But when my relationship with you ended - that was the first time I had to come to terms with being alone. Maybe I'm not over you and maybe I'm not happy, but if I continue to depend on people to keep me happy, then I never will be. All this is for the best, contrary to what you or I might think right now."

When she paused, it was Micah's turn to kiss the back of her hand. "There isn't any bad blood between us, and there never will be. You're fine from the looks of it, and hopefully I'll be able to be like that one day."

"Let me help you, Ellie."

She got to her feet. If he left first, she knew she'd stay in the coffee shop until closing time, thinking about all the things she should've said and all the things she should've done. Ellie didn't want anymore regrets than she already had - she didn't need more misery than she already felt. She wanted to have the last word, and she wanted that last word to mean resolution for her.

"If I start looking for help, I'm going to start depending again. Finding myself and what I want - it's something I have to do on my own."

"Is this goodbye forever then?" His voice shook.

"Goodbyes are only forever if you want them to be. Do you want this to be forever?"

"Fuck no."

She laughed - her first real laugh in what felt like years. "I love you so fucking much, Micah."

When she turned to walk away, Micah reached for her, his fingers wrapping around her wrist. "And how do you mean that, Ellie?"

She winked. "I mean it however you want me to mean it."

That - that felt like a start to resolution.

• • •

a/n: and so the final chapter of paper hearts!! oh boy has this been a ride, but there wasn't a single moment that i didn't enjoy. i cannot believe i actually managed to complete this story, but now that i have, i couldn't be more proud of where it's come. and i hope you guys like this ending too! if you're curious about the first ending for the story, here's a summary of it: isla and micah were still going to get married, but ellie was going to go to the wedding and micah was going to leave isla at the alter and instead profess his love for ellie. but, there's a reason i didn't go through with that ending - it's absolutely horrendous. first of all, hasn't isla been through enough already?? second of all, ellie and micah just don't belong together. not because micah was in truly in love with isla, but because they're not good for each other. gavin and hannah from the beginning of this story cheated on their significant others and when they got into a relationship, it didn't last. ellie and micah have done the same thing, so it wouldn't be right for them to have that kind of happily-ever-after. i just wanted everything to come full circle, and i think it did. BUT! if you are unhappy with isla and micah ending up together, never fear!! isla, just like mitchell, is going to have her own story called Broken Hearts so stay tuned for that! lemme know if you'd like to see it posted! with that being said, thank you all so so so much for reading. i'm going to miss this story, and i hope you all will too, but this story wouldn't be where it is without you guys constantly supporting it and supporting me. thank you all for being such kind, wonderful readers - i feel blessed every day to have some of the best readers in the world! thank you for sticking around and being amazing <3